MY FAIRY GODFATHER
Collected Short Stories

by

Rebecca D. Bruner

Cover Photograph by Sharon L. Hoff

DEDICATION

To Sheryl Kelly:
Your encouragement and faith in my talents
have spurred me on from the very beginning.
Thanks for introducing me to great books as a kid,
for praying for me without ceasing,
for reading and offering constructive criticism on my work,
and most of all for urging me to persevere in my quest
to find my voice and tell His stories.
Love always, Beck.

CONTENTS

My Fairy Godfather   1

The Red Unicorn   5

Haley's Horrible Day   29

Working the Polls   37

A Heart Like Mary's   41

Megan and Zoe   49

The Sirens' Sword   57

Everything He Needed to Say 107

About the Author   111

ACKNOWLEDGEMENTS

This book is a collection of shorter fiction and creative non-fiction pieces written since that fateful hour, almost eight years ago, when I first screwed up enough courage to begin submitting my stories for publication and enduring the inevitable ordeal of rejection letters and rewrites. Many of these stories represent my first real successes, those pieces that were (finally) accepted for publication in online magazines, or anthologies from small presses.

"Haley's Horrible Day" first appeared in the online magazine, *Teenage*, from Double Edged Press, in 2007. "The Red Unicorn" was published in *Mindflights*, Double Edged Press' speculative fiction e-zine, edited by Selena Thomason, in 2008.

"The Sirens' Sword" originally appeared in *The Cross and the Cosmos,* a Christian speculative fiction e-zine edited by Frank Luke and Glyn Shull, in the fall of 2011.

"Megan and Zoe" was first released in Hidden Brook Press' 2011 Christmas anthology, *Celebrating Christmas with Memories, Poetry and Good Food*, edited by Donna Goodrich.

"Everything He Needed to Say" was featured in the *Life Lessons from Dads* anthology from Write Integrity Press, edited by Suzanne Williams and Tracy Ruckman which came out in June, 2012.

"Working the Polls" and "A Heart Like Mary's" were adapted from blog posts which I published on my website, www.rebeccabruner.wordpress.com, in November and December of 2012, and "My Fairy Godfather" appears in this collection for the first time.

I'd like to extend my heartfelt thanks to all those editors over the years who have deemed my stories worthy of their notice, and to all those readers who have derived joy from my writing.

My Fairy Godfather

A fledgling writer's inner child pays a visionary call upon C.S. Lewis, her favorite departed literary mentor, in his lodgings up in heaven.

Uncle Jack sat before the fire in a great, wing-backed arm chair with a book in his lap, a pipe in his mouth and a drink at his elbow. I crept in quietly over the soft carpet, which shimmered like spun gold in the dancing firelight, and curled up at his feet.

A smile spread across his broad, honest face. "Do you want to hear a story, my dear?" he asked.

"I love your stories, Uncle Jack." His stories had been the constant companions of my childhood. They taught me joy and freedom when I was being educated to believe in nothing but legalism and cheerless discipline. His books had set my heart free from demerits and dress codes and straight lines; free to run barefoot through the grass and to feel the warmth of Lion kisses on my face. But I had not come to hear a story. "There's something I must tell you."

"What is it?" He peered down at me over the thick, black rims of his large, round spectacles.

"Do you remember how you felt when you read George Macdonald's book, *Phantastes*, for the first time? Like a door had been opened, the door into Fairy Land,

and through it you could glimpse eternity? In *The Great Divorce*, you wrote about how Macdonald's stories moved your heart and drew you to God. You saw holiness in them, though you didn't recognize it as such in the beginning."

"Yes." He smiled wistfully.

"That's how I've always felt about you. I've always thought of you as my godfather, my fairy godfather, if you will. You opened my eyes to another world. You were my spiritual mentor, and my companion, and a very great comfort to me, especially since I had no father of my own at the time."

"One far greater than I is the Father to the fatherless," he reminded me.

"Yes, I understand that, but what I wanted to tell you is thanks for letting Him speak through you."

The fragrance of his pipe filled the room like incense. "The pleasure was all mine," he sighed.

We sat gazing into the fire, silent for a while in a mutual reverie, remembering the places and the people once more: Narnia, Archenland, Calormen, the Lone Islands, Aslan's country. They were places created in his heart which I had been fortunate enough to visit only because he had shown the way. Even better were the people: first of all Aslan (who else?) and Peter, Edmund and Susan, Caspian and Reepicheep, Rillian, Eustace, Jill and Puddleglum, Hwin, Bree, Shasta and Aravis, and Tirian and Jewel, all of them dear, dear friends, because he had introduced us. And of course, I could never forget the lovely, joyful, golden-haired girl, more dear to me than a sister, Queen Lucy the Valiant.

I rested my head against his knee and said, "When I grow up, I want to be a writer, just like you."

"Just like me?" he chuckled, "Heavens, I should

hope not!"

I looked up at him, my brow furrowing in disappointment.

"My dear, you must find your own voice. You must follow His path for you, not another's. And you must have patience. In time, He will give you a voice both strong and fair and, perhaps, young readers who will one day become your very own godchildren. But even if no one ever reads a word you write, remember you already have an indispensable part in His story. Your name is in His book, you know."

I drew his hand to my lips and kissed it, tears of joy welling in my eyes. "Thank you," I whispered.

"You know," he said, patting my hand, "I should also thank you."

"For what?"

"Well, I never had a little girl, but in you, I have a posterity of sorts. You're like a granddaughter to me."

"Probably a great-granddaughter."

"Goodness, has it been so long?"

"I'm afraid so. But your name is well remembered. Your words live on."

He snorted derisively. "What is poetic immortality in comparison with that which is Life indeed?"

I couldn't help but smile.

"But back to the point," he went on, "you have been the best audience any writer could ever hope for, someone whose heart was inspired by my words."

"Someone who saw the same truth?"

"Precisely. We are friends, though from afar. I've shown you the beauty and wonder that I saw and you have loved it, just as I did."

I smiled. "The pleasure was all mine."

"My words have blessed you, and your warm

admiration has blessed me, and in all of this God's heart is blessed because it was really His story all along."

I looked up at him fondly. "Thank you again, dear Uncle. I look forward to meeting you in person, and not just on paper."

"I'll tell you something, my dear. I and some of my friends (Tolkien, Macdonald, Bunyan, and Bede, to name a few) have a little group that meets to read all sorts of things aloud. Once you've joined us here, in my Father's house, why don't you come and share one of your stories with us?"

I clapped my hands, delighted by the prospect of one day visiting that great Inklings meeting in the sky. "Oh, Uncle Jack! There's nothing I'd like more."

"And now, good night, dear heart. You will find your voice, no doubt, and I shall look forward to hearing your stories, because they will really be His, and His stories are all well worth hearing. Now run along." He shooed me off, like a child who has stayed up past her bedtime.

"Good night, Uncle Jack," I whispered, lingering a moment longer, "and God bless you."

The Red Unicorn

The urgent clanging of bells wrenched Mirrin from slumber. Weary from gathering medicinal herbs in the thin, mountain air, she had only meant to rest a moment, but long shadows now stretched behind the trees. She scrambled to her feet, and ran to the edge of the cliff.

Her eyes widened with horror as she looked down to see the people of her village scurrying in panic. The odor of burning thatch smote her nostrils. Armed men with torches swarmed through the streets, setting houses ablaze. A swelling crowd fled in the direction of their lord's fortress, seeking refuge, while the church bells pealed the alarm. Mirrin stifled a sob.

She hoped desperately that her own parents were among the throng flooding into the keep, though she knew joining them would be impossible. The climb down the cliff was treacherous. Long before she could reach the bottom, Rillec the Wolf and his mob would have laid siege to the castle.

Trembling, she peered into the forest. The fair folk were rumored to haunt these woods. Mortals who saw such creatures were seldom seen again. The few who returned would sigh their lives away, eaten up with an insatiable longing for just another glimpse of an elf or unicorn.

Once more, she stared down into the angry flames. No matter what might be lurking in those woods, it couldn't be more dangerous than the band of outlaws below.

Mirrin turned and fled into the forest's deepening gloom. She ran until her feet were raw and her lungs on fire. She was on the verge of collapse, when the girl glimpsed the lime-whitened walls of a humble cottage in the moonlight. Mirrin staggered forward, and knocked at the door.

*****

Firelight danced over the strange woman's face, revealing a beauty worn away by years of care. Mirrin's gaze wandered upward to the stone chimney behind her hostess. A great, black shield, emblazoned with a rampant, red unicorn hung above the mantelpiece. The image glowed like molten metal in the firelight. Mirrin could picture the creature shaking his proud head in fury and impaling his enemies with his terrible horn.

She shivered and studied the woman with growing apprehension. A shield that magnificent didn't belong in a peasant's hut. The scowling, old woman didn't look much like a fairy, but perhaps Mirrin should not have been so quick to accept her hospitality, or to tell her own story....

"You are very lucky," the woman said, "though you likely haven't the wit to see it."

Her reproachful tone startled Mirrin.

"Perhaps you think you'd be safer with your loved ones..." The old woman shook her head. "They're already as good as dead. Rats in Rillec's trap."

Mirrin's voice quavered. "What will he do to

them?"

"Rillec is not called 'Wolf' for nothing. He's cunning and tenacious. He'll assail the castle with catapults and flaming arrows. His men will dig under the foundation until your lord's fortress crumbles around him. If that should fail, he will wait for winter. Starvation and disease will prey upon your people, until they have no more strength to resist."

"Is there no hope?" Mirrin's eyes glistened with unshed tears.

The women gazed up at the shield with a wistful expression. "If Rillec were challenged by the Knight of the Red Unicorn, he might be defeated."

"Would Rillec really agree to a single combat?"

"He has a score to settle with the Unicorn Knight. He'll accept the challenge. Pride will drive him to his doom."

"Even if he were killed, would his followers lift the siege?"

"Once their leader is dead, Rillec's men will desert or fight amongst themselves."

Mirrin studied the fantastic shield. "Do you think the Unicorn Knight would agree to come and help us?"

"That may depend upon you."

"How do you know all this?"

Her hostess leaned back and stared into the embers. In a rich, melodic voice she began to tell her tale.

*****

Long ago, my father was the steward of a powerful duke. After years of faithful service, he was his most trusted advisor.

The duke had provided apartments for our family

within his court. I spent many happy hours chasing about the duke's castle as a prattling tot with my two brothers whom I called "Elwick" and "Will." Elric, my elder brother, soon outgrew this childish epithet, but I stubbornly persisted in mispronouncing my younger brother's name for years, because I knew how it annoyed him. I was often the victim of Will's cunning pranks, and I did what I must to settle the score. Despite these squabbles, we loved each other dearly, though our carefree childhood days passed by all too quickly.

In time, our well-beloved duke died, and all his subjects mourned his passing. His son, Lord Mavorin, assumed his father's seat. He then bestowed knighthood on my elder brother and took my younger brother as his squire.

Duke Mavorin held a great feast and called his nobles to swear fealty to him. Only Sir Othric, who had once vainly arisen against the old duke, dared to spurn the invitation. In the midst of the feast, Othric's herald appeared, denouncing the young duke as a bastard, and defying him to prove in battle that he was worthy of his dukedom.

Many of the vassals were eager to demonstrate their loyalty and valor by defending their duke's claim. Others seemed to be weighing the young duke's mettle. Would their new liege lord prove himself worthy to be feared as well as honored?

Duke Mavorin gathered one hundred of his knights and retainers, including my two brothers, and rode out against Sir Othric. The morning they departed, they were a fair sight in their shining armor and bright livery.

—

I kissed my brothers goodbye, and bade them ride forth to glory! Being only a naïve girl, I found it thrilling to imagine them going off to battle, and I envied them.

My father did not share my enthusiasm. As the steward, he had to manage all the duke's affairs in his absence, and he was now worried for both his sons.

I watched him pace the stone floor in his study, peering out the high tower window for any messenger bearing tidings of the battle, but none came.

After many days, he saw riders approaching in the distance. He called me to him, since my young eyes could better discern the standard they carried. The wind spread the banner so I could clearly recognize a white charger on a sable field, my elder brother's coat of arms.

I flung my arms about my father's neck.

"They are safe!" I exclaimed, "Elric is safe."

"Why do they ride under Elric's banner, and not the duke's?" he pondered.

We raced down to the courtyard. I embraced Elric with joy, but he had little time to speak with me. My father began interrogating him about the duke and the battle at once.

"Perhaps it would be best to speak of this in private," my brother suggested, and they retired to my father's study.

I turned to my younger brother. "Brave Will," I exclaimed, "tell me of all your valiant deeds!"

My brother's face was grim. "Be thankful that you were born a maid, and not a man," he said. I thought he was mocking me, but there was no mirth in his tone. "You will never find yourself face to face with a man who means to kill you." He turned and walked away, leaving me dumbfounded.

I ran to catch up with him.

"I'm sorry!" I cried.

"You know nothing of battle, Glynnis," he snapped. "It's not a matter for jest."

"What happened?" I asked earnestly.

"Othric's men ambushed us. We were riding to meet them in open battle, but they surprised us on the road." His face darkened at the memory. "Have you ever seen a man slain? Do you know what it's like to watch someone bleed his life away?" His words were bitter, almost accusing. I did not know what to say.

He went on, "Othric has taken Duke Mavorin hostage. He demands a ransom in exchange for his safe return. Elric suspects this was his intent from the outset." Will lapsed into a sullen silence. I could not guess how my brother had been so profoundly altered. He seemed quite unlike the light-hearted prankster I remembered.

Since I could learn no more from Will, I rushed to my father's study to discover what my elder brother had told him. Father perused the letters Elric had brought, and the color drained from his face. I turned to my brother.

"Is it true that Sir Othric is holding the duke for ransom?" I asked.

"Indeed, it is," my father interjected, "and the amount he demands for his release is twice the annual income of all Lord Mavorin's lands put together. We cannot possibly raise such a sum."

"What will we do?" I asked, my head spinning. Only a few weeks before, our family had been secure.

My father's position had seemed unshakable. Now the whole world was turning upside down.

"I shall challenge Sir Othric to single combat," my father announced. "If I defeat him, he will trouble us no more, and the duke will be set free."

Elric and I exchanged anxious glances.

"Do you really think that's wise, my lord?" he asked.

"It is the honorable thing to do."

Elric held his peace. If our father was convinced this was his duty, nothing could dissuade him.

My father called for Giles Clarric, the man who had always served as his secretary. He had watched me and my brothers grow up, and he loved us like an uncle. Though the devoted secretary would never breathe a word of his concern, I noticed him biting his lip as my father dictated his challenge.

Othric soon responded, arriving with an entourage of squires, pages, grooms, and guards. He also brought Duke Mavorin, who was bound and blindfolded like a common criminal.

Until that day, I had only seen tournament jousting, where knights try their skills and compete for prizes. I had never before witnessed a contest like this, where my own father's life and the future of my home hung in the balance.

I sat alone in our family's box, since both my brothers were assisting our father. Sir Othric rode up before me and saluted. I turned away, making no reply. I could hear him laughing behind my back.

"You'll speak gently to me before long," he said as he rode off.

Soon, my father came to salute the box.

11

"May heaven smile upon you, Father," I said. There was no time for long good-byes.

My father and Sir Othric took their places in the lists. The flag signaled them to start, and they rode toward each other at full speed, each one's deadly lance leveled at his opponent's breast. At the first stroke, Sir Othric threw my father from his horse. He struggled to gain his feet, but Othric bore down upon him with a naked broadsword. Under the rain of his blows, my father fell, never to rise again. It was the first time I had witnessed a joust to the death, and it was my own father who had fallen.

A wild shriek escaped from my lips. Will's angry words throbbed in my ears, "Have you ever seen a man slain?" Then the blackness swallowed me, and I fell to the ground.

"Are you well, my lady?" a low voice murmured.

Gradually, the pounding in my temples abated, and I became aware of someone's arm about my shoulders. I opened my eyes. As the haze in my head began to clear, I realized with a start that it was Sir Othric himself! I pulled away from him, and nearly swooned again.

"Leave me alone!" I screamed. "How dare you touch me?"

"I had to help a lady in distress," Othric replied with a smirk. He bowed and departed.

Shuddering, I staggered to my feet and hurried to join my brothers at our poor father's side. Hearts heavy with grief, we bore his body away and laid him to rest in the churchyard. He had lived and died a man of honor, but now his labors were at an end.

Ours, however, were just beginning. Almost before

the last shovel of earth was poured into my father's grave, Othric sent a new demand for ransom. He threatened to kill the duke if Elric, who was now steward, did not comply with his terms.

I fought off an eerie sense of foreboding, as my brother called for the secretary and responded with another challenge to single combat. My brother was a strong knight in the flower of his youth. He would surely fare better against Othric than my father had.

Elric himself shared my apprehensions. Before his bout with Othric, he fastened our father's spurs to young Will's heels and knighted him in the duke's name, thus ensuring that he could succeed him as steward.

Once again, the two combatants took their places in the lists. Elric fought fiercely, deflecting Othric's lance, and piercing his armor on the first pass. On the second pass, both lances were splintered by the impact as the knights collided.

While their attendants hurried to bring replacements, I got a good look at Elric. He appeared winded, but still strong. I began to hope that perhaps he would defeat the despicable knight.

On the next pass, Elric was swept out of the saddle. He hit the ground hard, and when he made no move to rise, I knew that he had taken his death wound. Will ran to him, and removed his helmet. He searched in vain for signs of life. With a heavy heart I watched him close Elric's eyes.

My throat grew tight. Hot tears trickled down my cheeks. I grasped the arms of my chair, my back like steel.

Meanwhile, Othric had commanded that Duke

Mavorin be brought before him. He drew a dagger with which to execute our wretched lord. The duke's handsome face seemed peaceful, despite the threat of impending death. Suddenly, my younger brother pushed between Othric and the duke. They exchanged words I could not hear, then Othric put up his dagger and his guards led the duke away. I sighed with relief. For the moment, Duke Mavorin had been spared. Then, Othric rode up to greet me. I braced myself for his onslaught.

"How fare you now, my haughty maid?" he asked. "Who will defend your virtue when all your kinsmen and your lord sleep in the churchyard?"

His words made my skin crawl. The blood pounded in my ears. I drove my nails into my palms to keep from swooning, lest I give him another excuse to lay his bloody hands on me.

To the churchyard we bore poor Elric's body, and laid him to rest. As Will and I observed the funeral rites, I had the uncanny sensation that we were reenacting my father's burial.

When it was over, I sat beside my young brother in the study which was now his. I took his hand.

"Must you challenge Othric now? I don't think that I could stand to lose you as well."

He smiled. "Never fear, Glynnis. Fortune is a fickle mistress, but her wheel does bring some up, even as others are brought down. Only a month ago, if you had told me I would soon become a knight, I'd have said you were joking. But now I am one.

"I never dreamed of becoming lord steward myself and yet, here I am. Perhaps fortune will continue to smile upon me, and I will find a way to defeat Sir

Othric, even though others have failed."

He looked so serene in the face of mortal danger. After witnessing the death of his nearest kinsmen, my younger brother was being called upon to assume responsibilities far beyond his years. Manhood had been thrust upon him too soon. Before long, he would risk his life in the lists, and I wanted him to know how much I appreciated his sacrifice, so I called him by his proper name.

"I pray you are right, Rillec." I said.

That night, I could not sleep. As I lay brooding, I was startled by knocking at my chamber door. I quickly threw my mantle about me, lit a candle, and pulled the door open a crack.

There in the passageway stood Giles Clarric, the secretary. I knew not why he should be there at such a time of night, but his face was grave.

"Master Clarric! What's wrong?" I asked.

"My Lady Glynnis, you must flee from here at once," he whispered.

"What do you mean? Why?"

"Not an hour ago, the lord steward, your brother, dictated to me a message for Sir Othric."

"Well, of course he has to challenge him..."

"This was no challenge, but a proposition. If Othric will depart in peace, Lord Rillec has offered to become his vassal. To sweeten the bargain, he has promised Othric your hand in marriage along with your dowry."

I was appalled. I did not want to believe him, but I knew Master Clarric too well to doubt his word. Suddenly, Rillec's serenity in the face of danger took on a sickening aspect. He had been confident, not that fortune would smile upon him, but that he could contrive a way of escape for himself.

"I am glad," the secretary continued, "that your father did not live to see his own son behave like such a coward. It would have broken the good man's heart."

"What of the duke?" I asked, remembering Rillec's urgent conversation with Othric in the lists. Had my brother merely been playing for time?

"The steward has given Duke Mavorin up for dead. Othric may do with him what he will."

"This is horrible!"

"Yes, my lady, and I beg you to make haste. The message will undoubtedly be delivered to Sir Othric by daybreak."

"But what should I do?"

"Fly, my lady, and God give you speed." With that, he hurried down the passage and out of my sight.

Of all the horrors that had befallen me, this was the hardest to bear. Though I had lost my father and Elric, I would always treasure their memories in my heart. But Rillec had plotted to deliver me into the bosom of his foe. Now that I knew my brother was capable of such cruelty, even my fondest memories of him would be tainted forever.

Feeling desperate and friendless, I disguised myself in mail which had been poor Elric's, and stole out of the castle with only my horse for a companion.

My own brother had betrayed me, where could I turn for aid? Hoping to get as far from home as possible, I fled into the mountains. I soon found myself lost in this very wood.

At length, I reached a clearing where I could glimpse the stars. My bones were aching and I was too weary to care what would become of me. I dropped from the saddle onto the smooth turf at the foot of a tree, and cast my helmet aside. Clasping Elric's shield to my chest like a blanket, I fell asleep.

I was awakened with a start by the terror-stricken neighing of my horse. I hardly remembered where I was, or why. The stars had almost disappeared, and the sky was growing lighter. I vividly remember the wild look in my horse's eyes, her ears laid flat against her head in fear.

I tried to soothe her, but she bolted away into the forest. Whatever had terrified her was rapidly approaching. The earth shook beneath me, and the sound of galloping hoof beats echoed through the trees.

I struggled to my feet and raised my shield. I forgot to draw my sword, though such weapons were impotent against the mighty creature who now thundered into view.

He was a unicorn, but one unlike any I had ever heard tell of. He was enormous, as tall and broad-chested as the strongest war horse. A great dark horn protruded from his brow. His mane and tail were long and wild, flowing about him like a restless wind. As the light grew stronger, I realized that his coat was not white, but red, a deep, rich sorrel, such as I had never seen on any living beast.

At the sight of him, an intense, almost painful longing stirred within me. I sank to my knees in fear and awe, thinking that to be riven through the heart by his mighty horn would not be a bad ending. I could think of no better way to die than to be slain by one so majestic, so beautiful.

The mighty beast checked his mad career toward me. Snorting, stamping and shaking his mane, he began to canter in a wide circle around me. I remained frozen where I knelt, hardly daring to breath. The marvelous creature drew nearer in ever tightening circles.

The unicorn slowed to a stop, lowering his great head to my face. A spicy, invigorating scent hung about him. The warmth of his breath and the velvet of his muzzle caressed my cheek and neck. I sat frozen in wonder, half fearing he might suddenly rear up and trample me.

To my astonishment, the wild thing dropped to his knees and gently laid his great head in my lap. I could feel my tears welling, as I looked down into his solemn eyes. I, who had been left utterly friendless, had now finally found a friend. I had been driven from my birthplace, but I had the strange feeling that I had, at last, come home.

I laid down my shield, and began to stroke his fiery mane, and recount to him all my sorrows. Though he spoke no word, I could see in his eyes that he understood all I said.

I wept upon the unicorn's noble neck.

"When my own flesh and blood has betrayed me, who will protect me?" I cried.

The unicorn pressed his soft nose to my cheek. Then, with a mighty snort, he rose to his feet. Lowering his head, he struck the device on my shield with the tip of his horn. A blood red stain spread forth from it to cover the rampant stallion, dyeing the snow white charger crimson. Then he etched a new mark onto the shield's face. When he had finished, it bore the perfect image of a red unicorn, as it does unto this day. He had forever marked me as his own.

—

He stamped his hoof, and nickered, nodding his head and looking at me with expectation. Suddenly I understood that the unicorn was offering to be not only my friend, but my champion.

I ran to him, flinging my arms about his neck, and burying my face in his beautiful coat. He nuzzled my hair affectionately, and then pushed me towards the helmet and shield lying nearby, urging me to take these up once more. I donned my brother's helmet and slid the wonderful shield onto my arm. I clambered onto his great back, and we were on our way.

It was all I could do to hold on, as he galloped through the dense wood. I clutched at his mane with both hands, and drove my knees into his sides. To fall at such a speed would have surely meant my death, yet nothing had ever felt so thrilling.

The rising sun transformed the tree tops into a glowing canopy of green. When we reached the narrow road which had brought me to the forest, the great unicorn careened down the path like a mountain goat, barely checking his speed as it wound down the steep hillside. The trees melted into a shimmering blur as we sped past.

We raced on until we reached the castle of the duke. The unicorn charged into the lists, just as the sun reached its zenith. An awe-struck hush fell upon the crowd as we entered the arena.

I remember the startled look on Rillec's face as we rode past. He was surrounded by assistants as he reluctantly donned his armor. Since he could no longer use me to bargain with, he was apparently being forced to fight Othric. He was whiter than a sheet.

Pacing back and forth astride his horse, Sir Othric

railed against Rillec's cowardice and demanded a more worthy opponent. The red unicorn snorted and stamped his hooves. Othric turned about in amazement to see a knight clad in the armor of a dead man astride an enchanted steed. I saw him swallow hard, then lower his visor and level his lance.

He charged toward us with his spear pointed at my breast and, for a moment, I could almost sympathize with Rillec's fear. I raised my shield, and clutched the unicorn's mane.

The great, red unicorn lowered his head. He sped toward Othric, his deadly horn aimed at the knave's heart. The impact rang in my ears and jarred my teeth as his horn pierced the knight's armor. He drove it clear through Othric's body, sweeping him off the back of his horse with the force of the blow. He shook his proud head, and Sir Othric fell to the ground, lifeless.

A mighty cheer went up from all the duke's supporters. Othric's entourage retreated in haste, lest the fiery beast turn upon them next. They evaporated like fog in the heat of the sun. I was not certain who freed the duke, but the next thing I knew, he was coming toward me as I sat astride the magnificent unicorn.

He bowed low, saying, "Great champion, I am deeply in your debt. You and your noble beast have delivered me. How can I repay you for your valiant deed?"

At that very moment, I saw Rillec approaching. He, too, bowed down saying, "We, his subjects, are abundantly grateful to you for rescuing our beloved lord, Duke Mavorin."

I seethed with rage. Rillec had planned to abandon

his duke to death, yet now, believing his secret was safe, he expected to resume his role as steward.

I pulled off my helmet. My golden hair fell down my back. The spectators caught their breath as they recognized me at last. I pointed at Rillec.

"Coward! You tried to sell me to Othric to save your own neck. You were too afraid to fight in your duke's defense." Turning to the duke, I said, "My lord, don't be fooled by his innocent face. Your *honest* steward is no more than a wolf in the guise of a lamb!"

Rillec's jaw dropped in shock. For a moment he stood dumb, staring at me and the red unicorn. Then, shaking his fist, he shouted, "I swear, you'll pay for this Glynnis, you and your bloody beast!"

Before the duke could speak a word, Rillec had fled. He vaulted into his saddle and raced away like a hunted animal. The duke sent forth men to search for him, but he could not be apprehended. After many years, rumors reached us of Rillec the Wolf, an outlaw who had gathered a band of mercenaries and begun to terrorize the lands round about. His followers were all outlaws who had been driven from the society of honorable men.

*****

Mirrin broke in, "This is the same Rillec who has besieged my lord's castle?"

Glynnis nodded.

"And you are the Red Unicorn Knight?"

"I was once. I have not yet told you the end of my tale."

Mirrin held her peace as Glynnis continued.

*****

The courtiers were jubilant over the defeat of Sir

Othric and the rescue of their beloved duke. They decked me and my unicorn in garlands of flowers, and prepared a magnificent feast.

I was half afraid that the fearsome beast would lash out against the crowd of adoring strangers which now encircled him. To my surprise, he behaved like a gentle palfrey, graciously accepting the adoration of all. He seemed content to abide in the best stall of the duke's stable.

The duke spoke again and again of rewarding me for my valor. He made me sit beside him at the high table. I could not remember any meal so sumptuous. The roast pig, the pigeon pies, the cakes, the wine were all the best I'd ever eaten. But then, bread and water would have tasted heavenly to me that day.

My heart exulted both because of the feat that my unicorn and I had achieved, and because I had returned to the haven of my home. The only reward I wished from the duke was a place in his court, though none of my kinsmen remained to serve him. I took a sip of my wine and summoned my courage to ask this of him, when he suddenly stood up to address the assembly.

"Good people, I owe my life to this lady." Motioning me to stand, he continued, "By her valor, she delivered me from the hand of the foul Othric, and exposed the treason of Rillec, who might have ruined me."

The crowd roared their approval, and I blushed with pleasure. He went on, "Such service is worthy of the highest honor I can bestow." Taking my hand, he dropped on one knee, and said, "Lady Glynnis, will you be my bride?"

The room erupted in applause. I stood,

dumbfounded. Since childhood, I'd lived in awe of Lord Mavorin, watching him grow to manhood with a mixture of adoration and envy. It seemed that he lived in a world of unattainable prestige. He was destined to become the master over everything in my sphere of experience.

Now, he offered to make me mistress of all his dominion. The life of ease I'd coveted could be mine. What's more, he had the means to protect me from hardship or danger. Having lost all my kinsmen, I thought he could provide me with the security I lacked. This seemed to be the answer. I need never again fear being cast forth from my home if I became his duchess.

"What say you, Lady?" the duke asked softly. Still too overwhelmed to speak, I nodded my acceptance.

We were married at once, to the great delight of the courtiers. They escorted us from the banquet to the chapel with singing and dancing. The merry making went on long past sunset, but at last the eventful day drew to a close. My lord carried me over the threshold of his chamber. I went to his bed a maid and arose the next morning a duchess.

I awoke to find that my lord had already arisen, for he had many affairs to set in order. I lay in bed pondering my new good fortune, until there came a gentle knock at the door.

The duke had sent a lady in waiting to attend me. Her name was Amilea. She was ten years older than I, and her demeanor was pleasant. I liked her at once.

She brought in an armload of magnificent garments, explaining that, since I was now a duchess, I needed clothes befitting a lady of such rank. From among the dresses, I selected a glorious gown of blue silk, embroidered with gold, and trimmed with ermine, and with it a beautiful cap of blue velvet, adorned with pearls. I had never even touched such finery before.

Amilea dressed me in my new attire and I gleefully stepped out onto the balcony to greet the morning. Looking down over the manor, I suddenly noticed a great commotion in the direction of the stables. Men were running from everywhere and shouting to one another.

For the first time, I thought of the red unicorn. What if the stables were ablaze and he were trapped? I knew I couldn't bear it if any harm came to him. Picking up my heavy skirts, I raced down to the stables, my gentlewoman calling after me in alarm.

Upon reaching the stables, I was relieved to discover that there was no fire.

"What's wrong?" I asked a groom as he raced past me.

"It's the unicorn, my lady," he cried over his shoulder. "He's gone mad!"

I rushed into the stable, to find the unicorn all in a lather, his wild eyes rolling. He was thrashing and kicking in every direction. Several grooms were trying to get close enough to throw a rope about his neck, but he swung his deadly horn at them and they were forced to back away.

I charged in, reaching out my hand and crying, "Be at peace, dear heart. I am here." At the sight of me, he bared his teeth and uttered a shriek. I tried to come nearer, but he shied away from me with loathing. So desperate was he to flee, that he turned his hind quarters to the stable wall and bludgeoned it with his hooves, until the boards snapped. Then he forced his way through the hole he'd broken in the wall, and raced into the wilds. I ran into the stall, peering through the hole in shock. With a bitter cry, I collapsed on a pile of straw, the tears streaming down my cheeks.

Soon, Amilea caught up to me. Gathering me in her arms, she raised me to my feet and guided me back to the duke's chamber. She sat me down, and laid a soothing hand on my shoulder.

"It's a mercy you weren't killed, my lady."

"He ran away from me!" I sobbed. "He couldn't stand the sight of me."

"I suppose it is to be expected, my lady," said the gentlewoman.

I stared up at her, bewildered.

"They say only a maiden can tame a unicorn," she explained.

Suddenly I realized the terrible truth. I had thoughtlessly broken faith with the red unicorn, prizing my own comfort and protection more than his devotion. When I had nowhere else to turn, I had put my trust in the mighty creature, but when a way to safeguard my own fortunes presented itself, I had been all too quick to seize it, never counting the cost. Like Rillec, I had sought my own safety at the expense of one who loved me.

"I should never have done it!" I moaned. "I want my unicorn back. I don't want to be a duchess."

"But you are a duchess, my lady, and there are some choices that cannot be undone."

A bitter truth, and how well did I know it!

Amilea went on, "The duke is a kind and noble gentleman. He deserves a good wife."

I was forced to admit she was right. Lord Mavorin

should not suffer for my folly.

*****

"And so what did you do?" Mirrin wondered.

"I lived as his wife for thirty-five years. In time, I learned to love him for himself instead of for the image of prestige and protection I had once idolized. Even so, my heart ached with longing for what I had lost. When my lord died four years ago our son succeeded him as duke. I hoped that, perhaps, now I was alone again, the red unicorn might return to me. So, with my son's leave, I came to live here in the forest."

Mirrin pitied the old woman for whom even the greatest pleasures of the ordinary world had been spoiled forever by a glimpse of the enchanted realm. Even a life of wealth and privilege had given her no satisfaction. She had left it all behind to live alone in a thatched hut, for nothing more than the hope of drawing near to the unicorn once again.

"And has he returned to you?" Mirrin asked.

Glynnis shook her head sadly. "I have seen him far off once or twice, and I have often heard him in the night. But no, he will not return to me. Only a maiden can tame the red unicorn." Glynnis looked at the young girl pointedly. Mirrin shifted in her seat and dropped her gaze.

"Have you stopped to wonder why you were so lucky? By pure chance, you were beyond the reach of Rillec and his men. Have you considered that perhaps you were spared for a reason?"

Mirrin frowned as she studied the lady's face. What did this woman expect from her? Then, all at once, she began to understand…

"It must be your decision, child. I can write letters

of recommendation to my son, the duke. You can start a new life as a serving woman in his house, and forget about your father and your mother, and the others you love who are trapped in Rillec's siege. Perhaps, in time, you will find an honest husband who will give you a home, and a family to replace the one you will have lost.

"Or you can take up the shield of the red unicorn. You can become the Red Unicorn Knight and by his help, deliver your family and your people, and put an end to Rillec the Wolf, once and for all.

"But I warn you, if you are not as you seem, a maiden chaste, confess it now, or he will surely trample you beneath his deadly hooves."

For a long while, Mirrin pondered the choice before her. She considered the life Lady Glynnis offered her as a serving woman in a duke's court where she would be provided for and assured of a position. She pictured the faces of her mother and father, trapped within the keep, waiting for starvation and sickness to prey upon them. She could turn her back on them and begin a whole new life in security and comfort. Or she could commit herself to become the red unicorn's knight and forever forsake the life of an ordinary woman.

She need not admit her cowardice to Lady Glynnis. She could lie to the old woman, and deny that she was a maid. But in her own heart she would always know that she had not been brave enough to deliver those she loved.

"I am a maiden," she declared at last.

*****

Mirrin pulled the heavy cloak about her shoulders. Bright stars glittered above the clearing that stretched before her. Pale moonlight reflected from the great black shield with the crimson unicorn which she clutched to her breast. Hardly daring to breathe, she strained her ears for the one sound she was both dreading and longing to hear: the approach of thundering hooves.

Haley's Horrible Day

Haley ran into the house and straight down the hall to her room.

"How was school?" her mom called after her.

"I don't want to talk about it," she replied, slamming the door and flinging her backpack to the floor. She flopped onto the bed and buried her face in the pillow. Seventh grade was turning into a disaster. At the end of last year, she, Caitlin, and Emily had promised to stick together when they went to Jr. High. They had all been good friends in grade school, but now the others seemed to think Haley wasn't cool enough for them.

Today, things had started going downhill at lunch.

Caitlin frowned as Haley sat down. "Isn't that the same lunch box you had last year?" she asked.

"Yeah. What's wrong with it?"

Caitlin speared a forkful of her salad. "Nothing...if you're in third grade," she answered.

"Hey," said Emily, setting down her tray and sliding in beside Haley. "Nice outfit."

"Thanks." Haley's face brightened.

"I'd love to have a blouse just like that," agreed Caitlin. "Where'd you get it?"

"It's a hand-me-down from my cousin."

"Well, at least she has good taste," Caitlin sniffed.

Emily asked, "How come you never get any new clothes?"

Haley's cheeks grew hot. Her tuna sandwich tasted like cardboard. She wished she knew how to make them stop. If only her family were really rich, she could buy a cool new wardrobe. Then maybe her friends wouldn't be embarrassed to be seen with her.

The bell rang and Haley hurried to the choir room. She was still upset as she found her seat in the soprano section, and it showed.

Sarah Dominguez sat down beside her, her deep brown eyes full of concern. "What's wrong?" she asked. "Are you okay?"

Before Haley had a chance to answer, Ms. Griggs motioned for the chorus to stand and begin warming up. Haley doubted Sarah would have really understood anyway.

She was feeling a little better by the time she got to Pre-Algebra. The bell rang, and Mr. Beatty went over the homework. He began calling people up to solve the hardest problems.

"Haley, could you please do number seventeen?"

Usually, she didn't mind going to the board, but today the teacher had asked for the one problem she had no clue how to solve.

"I totally didn't get that one," she admitted.

"Did anybody get number seventeen?"

The kids looked down at their desks hoping to avoid the teacher's gaze. Finally, at the back of the room, one hand went up.

"Mia," said Mr. Beatty, sounding a little surprised, "Do you want to come up and do the problem?" Mia

Carter was new. She had moved from another state after school had started. She wore braces and hardly ever spoke.

Mia stepped up to the board, and began solving the hardest problem in the homework. Haley was impressed. Mia didn't have much to say, but she was obviously very smart.

After math, Haley hurried down the hall to World Geography, her last class of the afternoon. She slid into her seat behind Caitlin, and next to Ian Woods, who greeted her with a smile and a wave. Haley responded with a shy nod.

Emily kept telling Haley that Ian liked her and might ask her out, if she played her cards right. Haley didn't feel quite ready to rush into romance, though she didn't dare mention that to her friends.

"Just be careful not to act like too much of a *brain*," Caitlin had advised her. "Everyone knows guys don't like girls that they think are too smart for them."

Haley suspected Caitlin felt that way, herself. Haley had always believed it was good to be smart, but lately, she'd noticed her friends trading embarrassed glances whenever she spoke up in class.

Just before the bell, Caitlin spun around and asked, "What did I miss yesterday when I was at the dentist?"

"We started a new unit on Africa. We're supposed to choose a country and write a research paper on it by next Friday," Haley explained.

"Oh, that's the worst," Caitlin moaned, as Emily plopped down in the seat beside her.

"I like research papers," said Haley, "They're interesting."

Caitlin rolled her eyes. "You are so weird!"

Emily came to her defense. "You shouldn't say that about Haley. That's perfectly normal...," then grinning, she added, "On her planet!"

The room erupted. Caitlin, Emily, Ian, and all the other kids were howling with laughter. Haley wanted to melt into a puddle under her chair. Just when she thought things couldn't get any worse, Ian held up his hand, spread the fingers into a "V" and said, "Live long and prosper." It was all she could do to keep from rushing out of the room.

Haley's eyes began to sting as she thought back over her horrible day. She punched the pillow, and brushed away a hot tear. She hated the way Caitlin and Emily were acting, but she desperately wanted their friendship. She felt weary and trapped. She let her head sink into the pillow's cool softness.

She heard a gentle knock at the door.

"What is it?" Haley muttered.

Her mom peeked in. "I was wondering if you'd like a snack."

Haley swung her legs over the edge of the bed, then trudged down the hall and into the kitchen.

"How 'bout some yogurt and an apple?"

"Whatever."

Mom bustled about collecting yogurt and spoons. Haley watched her push the apple slicer down over the fruit. Apple wedges fell away from the core like blooming petals. Haley sighed.

"Here we go," said Mom, laying the food out on the table and sitting down. She bit into an apple slice and chewed it in silence.

Haley took a spoonful of peach yogurt and swished it in her mouth. It felt cold and sweet and creamy on her tongue.

"Mom," she asked, "what do you do when your friends treat you like you're weird?"

Her mom frowned. "Hmmm…"

"I've known Caitlin and Emily forever, but now they act like I'm not cool enough for them."

"What are they doing?"

Haley recounted the whole terrible episode from geography.

"Mom, it was the most embarrassing moment of my life!"

"Oh, Honey." She shook her head. "Kids can be so cruel."

"Why do they have to act like that?"

"At your age, most kids feel unsure of themselves. Some try to build their own self-esteem by cutting others down."

Mom reached out and gently brushed Haley's brown hair back behind her ear.

"Sometimes, I wish I had a magic wand I could wave to let you skip over this messy season of life," Mom went on. "I'd say the magic words and poof; you'd be a beautiful young lady of twenty-one with a college degree, clear skin, and all the self-confidence in the world."

"That'd be nice."

"But you know something? Even if I had a magic wand, I wouldn't use it."

"Why not?"

"Because every new butterfly has to fight its way out of the cocoon all by itself. Only through that struggle can it develop the strong wings it needs to fly."

"You're saying I'm a butterfly?"

"Yep, and right now you're struggling hard to get out of the cocoon. One day you will fly. You'll be a mature, strong and beautiful young woman...."

Haley looked doubtful.

"I'm not just saying that because I'm your mom, either. You're a wonderful girl, Haley. You're smart and talented and funny. I've always known it, and someday other people will see it, too."

"I just wish I knew how to find those people."

Mom considered this as she took another bite of apple. "Well," she said, "you might start by looking for friends who are interested in the kind of things you *really* enjoy...."

Haley thought of Mia Carter, the new girl in her math class. Though she was pretty shy, she seemed really smart. Or maybe Sarah Dominguez, who sat next to her in Chorus. Sarah was unlike the kids Haley knew from grade school. She could speak Spanish, and she took the bus, but she and Haley had one thing in common; they both loved to sing.

"If you look hard enough, I'll bet you can find some people who will like you for who you are, and not who they want to make you. Remember, you're a butterfly. You don't have hang around with people who treat you like a caterpillar."

Haley nodded. She'd never really thought of herself as a butterfly.... She smiled as she imagined fluttering over a field of giant flowers on shimmering, purple wings. Horrible days like today didn't seem as bad when she recognized that they served a purpose. They were giving her the strength to fly.

Mom cleared the remnants of their snack from the

table. "It's about time for you to get going on your homework."

Haley roused herself from her day dream. "Do you know what happened to the school chorus roster?" she asked, "I want to call Sarah Dominguez."

"That sounds like a great idea…after you've finished your homework."

Haley smiled and rolled her eyes. She went back to her bedroom and pulled out her math book. Pre-algebra was not her favorite subject, but she could see how it, too, would help make her stronger.

She took out a piece of paper and wrote her name at the top. Before she began to work, she doodled a little butterfly in the margin.

Working the Polls

There is nothing like working the polls to put you in touch with all that is best and worst about Americans, though interacting with my fellow citizens was the last thing on my mind when I signed up to serve as a board worker for the primary election. When I learned I could earn a hundred bucks for a single day's work, I seized the chance. Since there is never money to spare in my budget, I had no doubt I could find ways to use the extra cash.

In the black pre-dawn of Election Morning, I stuffed all the food I needed for the day into a cooler and hopped into my car. My battery had been acting up for days. I turned the key and the engine reluctantly coughed to life. The dashboard display read January 1. Not a good sign, considering the fact that it was late August. I prayed that the car would start one more time to get me home at the end of the day.

It was 5:30 a.m. when I reported for duty at the recreation center of the tiny mobile home park that served as our polling place. Ours was one of three different precincts crammed into the same room, something bound to cause confusion, even though we posted a map to help the voters figure out where they were supposed to go.

The polls opened promptly at six o'clock, and

people began straggling in to exercise that most sacrosanct of American civil liberties, the right to vote. Once things started rolling, our jobs were fairly straightforward. Most of the voters were congenial and business-like, even so ridiculously early in the morning. We checked their IDs, then gave them their ballots. Once they were finished, we explained how to feed their ballots into the Insight machine, and then sent them on their way sporting "I voted today" stickers.

The job wasn't rocket science, and voter turn out was low, so we had plenty of time to chat. The most experienced members of our team were Becky and her sister RoJane, though health problems had kept Becky away for several years. She recounted to us the tales of her knee replacement surgeries and double mastectomy. Becky saw herself not as a cancer survivor, but as an overcomer. She said she enjoyed raising cockatiels and had rescued several baby hummingbirds.

The youngest member of our team was Miryam. She was a beautiful, black high-schooler, dressed in blue jeans and a Muslim headscarf. She was there to get credit in her government class. She had enjoyed playing softball, until she found herself on a team where she was clearly outclassed and ran the risk of getting hurt. At that point, she didn't find it fun anymore. She said she enjoyed reciting poetry at speech competitions.

Miryam was stationed near the door, trying to intercept the voters and help direct them to the correct precincts' tables, when this guy walked into the clubhouse. He was old and sinewy with an unhealthy tan and a mop of unruly white hair. One look at our young Muslim girl and he became loud and indignant. "I've never had to flip a coin to figure out where I was supposed to vote before!" he exclaimed. "I've been voting here for years."

Miryam, with her downcast, doe's eyes, attempted to show him the precinct map, but he became increasingly obnoxious. Soon, two older poll workers tried to intervene. I could understand the man's frustration, but he acted as though they were all there to give him a hard time. By the tone of his voice, I guessed he believed he was being funny. In reality he was making an ass of himself.

Finally, he was sent to my table. I put on my "happy waitress dealing with tipsy customer" voice, intentionally brightening my tone as I said, "If you'll just show me your ID, sir, we'll see if we can't find you over here."

He imparted a few more smart remarks as I checked his driver's license against the voter rolls and sent him down the table to get his ballot.

Before going off to vote, he made a crack about his T-shirt, which featured a pro-American symbol and sentiment. "Am I still allowed to be in here wearing this?" he asked.

Of course you are, I thought. *We just wish you'd shut up.*

When he finally finished voting and departed with his sticker, every poll worker in the room breathed a sigh of relief.

At the end of the day, RoJane took the memory cartridge from our Insight machine to election headquarters. As the rest of us went through our checklists and packed up, I mentioned to Becky that I was worried about my battery.

"RoJane can give you a jump as soon as she comes back," she said.

When I got to my car, the starter emitted only impotent clicks. I trotted back toward the clubhouse, intercepting RoJane in the parking lot just as she returned. She drove me back to the side street where I had parked.

"I don't have jumper cables," she said. "They're in Becky's car."

Just then, an elderly woman, hearing the noise from RoJane's engine, poked her head out of the trailer across the street.

"You wouldn't happen to have any jumper cables, would you?" I asked.

"Oh, sure," she replied. "I'll send my husband right out with them."

In five minutes, the old man stood between my open hood and RoJane's. He hooked up his cables, and I jumped into my car. I turned the key and the motor growled to life.

"Thank you so much," I said to both of them. I slammed the hood and drove off into the night, grateful for the kindness of strangers, and for a story to tell as I pondered the unforeseen blessings of a hard day's work in this odd yet wonderful place I call my home.

A Heart Like Mary's

Four Meditations

HUMBLE OBEDIENCE

I recently attended a restoration prayer workshop where a team of people asked the Lord to reveal my original design. Because we are all God's unique creations, each one of us reflects particular facets of His glory. One thing that surprised me was the revelation that I was intended to have a heart like Mary's.

During this past Advent season, I have spent a lot of time thinking about Mary and all the aspects of her heart that are revealed in the Christmas story. One of the most evident and important is her humble obedience.

It would have been easy for her to argue with the angel about God's plans for her life--"Hey, could you let God know that His timing here stinks? I've got a wedding to plan. Plus, travelling across the country in my third trimester of pregnancy is not part of my ideal birth plan."

But Mary didn't argue. She didn't demand that God provide explanations or contingency plans. She simply said, "Behold, the bondslave of the Lord. Be it done to me according to your word."

For me, it's too easy to want to know all of the why's, when's and wherefore's in my life. I struggle to trust that God truly knows better than I do. Instead of expecting God to provide me with all the answers, I need to learn to humble myself before Him and obey the things He asks of me, one day at a time, like Mary did.

FAITH

After the angel tells Mary that her relative Elizabeth is pregnant with John the Baptist, she goes immediately to the hill country of Judah to visit her.

As soon as Mary's greeting reaches her ears, Elizabeth's baby leaps in her womb, and she knows at once that Mary is carrying the Christ child. Then Elizabeth says, "And blessed is she who believed that there would be a fulfillment of what had been spoken to her by the Lord."

This is really significant because it is a direct contrast to how Elizabeth's husband, Zacharias, responded when he was visited by Gabriel six months prior and told that his wife would bear him a son. After getting such an amazing message from the angel, Zacharias asked, "How shall I know this for certain? For I am an old man and my wife is advanced in years."

As a consequence for his lack of faith, the angel tells him he will be unable to speak until the baby is born.

It's easy for me to say I have faith, but I tend to keep on questioning, like Zacharias. After years of barrenness, it was hard for him to believe his wife really would have a child.

After years of rejection, I can so easily slip into the frame of mind that assumes God has forgotten about me. That He doesn't really have a good plan for my writing and my future. That He hasn't heard my prayers.

Instead, I know He wants me to have faith like Mary's. Faith that doesn't doubt His goodness, or question His ability to bring about a future that is better than anything I could ask or think. Faith that hears tell of good news and starts walking that direction. Faith that not only prays for rain, but prepares the fields to receive it.

COURAGE

Mary must have been a very courageous young woman. She had to know that embracing God's plan for her life would involve terrible risks.

She risked the loss of her reputation, the rejection of her friends and family. She very nearly lost her future husband, who had every intention of breaking off their engagement until God intervened.

When her son was less than two months old, the prophet Simeon predicted that a sword would pierce even her own soul. Because Mary's child was destined to be the Savior of the world, she would be forced to endure unimaginable heartache, watching him suffer and die on a cross. In spite of all this, she did not refuse God's call on her life.

I have not been asked to experience anything like such agony, and yet I still find it difficult to courageously embrace the future God has for me. I want to take the safe, easy path, instead of boldly risking rejection. I want to hold my tongue, instead of saying what I know should be said. I want to hide my heart away, instead of loving others fearlessly and valiantly.

Lord, silence my fears and make me a woman of courage, like Mary.

JOY

"My soul exalts the Lord,
And my spirit has rejoiced in God my Savior.
For He has had regard for the humble state of His bondslave;
For behold, from this time on all generations will count me blessed.
For the Mighty One has done great things for me;
And holy is His name.
AND HIS MERCY IS UPON GENERATION AFTER GENERATION TOWARD THOSE WHO FEAR HIM.
He has done mighty deeds with His arm;
He has scattered those who were proud in the thoughts of their heart.
He has brought down rulers from their thrones,
And has exalted those who were humble.
HE HAS FILLED THE HUNGRY WITH GOOD THINGS;
And sent away the rich empty-handed.
He has given help to Israel His servant,
In remembrance of His mercy,
As He spoke to our fathers,
To Abraham and his descendants forever." Luke 1:46-55

In this poetic passage, Mary expresses incredible joy. The thing that I find interesting is that she is rejoicing, not only over the great things God is doing in her own life, but also about the bigger picture of God's work throughout history.

She talks about God having mercy on generation after generation. She is excited about his justice in bringing down the proud and the privileged, while exalting the humble and filling the hungry. The fact that God is keeping promises he made thousands of years before she was even born makes her joyful and excited.

Too often, my focus is so narrow. My joy in the Lord often hinges upon what I see Him doing in my life. I hardly give any thought to the bigger picture. I definitely don't write poetry praising him for His work throughout history and all over the globe.

Lord, teach me to have joy like Mary's. Help me to lift up your name because you are worthy, and not just because you've blessed me. Help me to rise above preoccupation with my own concerns and learn to rejoice in every aspect of who You are and what You have done, are doing, and will do.

Megan and Zoe
A Christmas Tale of Two Sisters

The last day of school before Christmas vacation, I was so excited I could hardly stand it. I skipped all the way home from the bus stop singing "Jingle Bells." Christmas was just around the corner!

I rushed into the house, flung my arms around my mom (who was on the phone) and gave her a big hug. "Only five more days `til Christmas!" I said.

"Shh," Mom said with a frown. She scrunched the receiver to her ear with her shoulder, while writing furiously on a notepad.

Even her grouchiness couldn't spoil my good mood. I kept humming as I pulled a packet of popcorn out of the pantry and put it in the microwave.

"No, don't worry about it," Mom told the person on the phone. "We'll go pick her up....All right. See you later." She hung up.

I grabbed the popcorn out of the microwave.

"Here," said Mom, taking it out of my hands.

"I can do it myself," I protested. I hate being treated like a baby. After all, I am in third grade.

"I just don't want you to get burned by the steam, Zoe." She opened the bag carefully, then grabbed a handful of popcorn.

"Hey, that's mine!"

"Well, you're going to have to bring it with you in the van."

"Where are we going?"

"We have to go to the airport to pick up Megan."

Oh no, not Megan! I had forgotten that she was coming today. No wonder Mom had seemed so grouchy.

Megan is my sister, but she never lived with us. She's eight years older than me, so when I was born, she was already as old as I am now. She lives in Minnesota. I live in Arizona. We really don't have anything in common. Except our dad. That's why she had to come stay with us for Christmas vacation but I wished she could have just stayed home. Megan never wants to play with me or do anything fun because all she thinks about is acting cool. If she tried any harder to be cool, she'd probably be frozen solid.

Before we moved from Minnesota to Arizona, Megan used to stay with us on weekends for "visitation" (which means that the judge said she had to come, even if she didn't want to). She spent most of her time in her bedroom. The only time she ever played with me was when Dad made her, and then all she wanted to do was play hospital.

"You be the doctor, I'll be the patient," she'd say, lying down on the sofa and closing her eyes. "And I'm in a coma."

I was almost 6 when we moved to Arizona, and Megan was 13. Because we lived so far away, she couldn't come on the weekends anymore, but I sure didn't miss having her around. Then Christmas break came and we got her for the whole two weeks! She didn't want to do anything. She didn't want to drive around and look at Christmas lights, or see Santa Claus at the mall. She didn't want to sing Christmas carols, or decorate sugar cookies, or make gingerbread houses. She didn't even want to watch *How the Grinch Stole Christmas.*

I was dreading the coming week as I sat in the backseat munching my popcorn.

"Mom," I said, "Why does Megan have to come?"

"We've been over this, Zoe. She gets to spend every other Christmas with Dad."

"But she'll ruin everything."

Mom sighed. She knew I was right but wouldn't admit it. "The fact is that Megan is your sister, and if there's one thing you have to learn during the holidays, it's how to tolerate difficult relatives."

"I wish we could have Christmas like last year, with just us."

"Well, honey, that's not the situation. Megan is coming, and we have to make the best of it."

Making the best of it didn't sound like much fun to me.

When we got to the airport, Mom parked the van and we hurried to baggage claim. We found the carousel where Megan's luggage was supposed to show up and stood around waiting. Finally, I caught sight of her. Her black hair matched her black, oversized coat and the black makeup around her eyes. A pair of earbuds dangled around her neck. She walked up to us and hiked her army-green canvas back pack higher on her shoulder. She looked from my mom's face to mine and then scanned the crowd of people behind us.

"Where's Dad?" she asked.

Rebecca D. Bruner

"He was planning to be here, but he got tied up at the office," Mom said with a stiff smile.

"Figures," said Megan. Without another word, she walked past us toward the baggage carousel.

"Merry Christmas to you, too," I muttered.

"Zoe," Mom frowned, "don't start. We're all trying to make the best of this, remember?"

I remembered, all right, but it wasn't going to be easy.

Two days before Christmas, Mom had to go in to work. Dad was home but he was "telecommuting," which means he was chained to his computer.

"I tell you what, girls, if you can occupy yourselves and not disturb me, I'll take you out for lunch," he promised. "What do you say?"

"I won't hold my breath," Megan muttered. I don't think Dad heard her.

He shut the door to the office and Megan went into the guest room. Pretty soon, I heard the sliding glass door open. I turned around to see Megan disappearing out back in her bathing suit! She couldn't be crazy enough to go swimming in December, could she? I hurried outside to see what she was up to.

She was lying on a lounge chair wearing sunglasses and a two-piece bathing suit. I shivered. I was cold even wearing my sweater and jeans.

"Aren't you freezing?" I asked.

Megan snorted. "Are you kidding? Back home, the lakes are frozen and the snow's as deep as your armpits. Living in Arizona is turning you into a wimp."

"I am not!" I said. "You know, if you love Minnesota so much, why don't you just stay there?"

"You think I want to come here? I'd rather spend

Christmas break hanging out with my friends, instead
of a snot-nosed, little brat who won't leave me alone!"
I never knew before that Megan hated being here
as much I hated having her around.
"But since I'm stuck in this God-forsaken desert,"
she went on, "I might as well come home with a tan."
She turned over on her stomach and pretended to
ignore me. I started walking along the edge of the pool
like a tightrope walker in the circus. Looking down, I
could see the sunlight dancing on the bright blue water.
"You know what I think?" I said, "I think you're
the wimp." I dipped my hand in the water and
splashed her.
She shrieked and sat up. "Cut that out!"
"I dare you to jump in!"
"No!"
"You said it wasn't even cold," I said, stepping
onto the diving board.
"It's not."
I started tightrope walking out toward the end of
the board.
"Megan's a chicken, Megan's a chicken." I flapped
my arms like wings and bounced up and down.
"Get off of there or you're gonna fall in, you little
freak, and don't expect me to rescue you."
"Don't worry about me," I said, "I know how to
swim." I stood tip toe on one foot and lifted the other
leg out behind me, spreading my arms like a ballerina.
"I mean it, Zoe. Get off!" she shouted.
"Make me," I started to say, when suddenly I lost
my balance. I wobbled for a moment, and then
splashed into the pool.
It was so cold, it took my breath away. My sweater

and jeans felt like they weighed a thousand pounds and my soggy tennis shoes made it really hard to kick. I held my breath as my head bobbed under the icy water.

The next thing I knew, there was a huge splash and Megan was dragging me to the side.

"Let me go," I tried to say, "I can swim," but my mouth was full of water. Finally, she hauled me out of the pool.

Dad stuck his head out the sliding glass door, looking worried. "What's going on?"

Megan and I lay panting on the cool deck.

"Are you two okay?" he asked.

"We're fine, Dad," Megan answered. "Zoe just thought it would be fun to go swimming."

"Are you crazy? It's the middle of December."

Megan looked at me and rolled her eyes. My teeth were chattering, but I started to giggle. Then Megan started giggling, too. Pretty soon we were both laughing so hard, we couldn't stop.

"Come in the house before you catch pneumonia!" Dad ordered.

In no time, we were bundled up in bathrobes and blankets in front of the fireplace. He switched on the gas log and went to make us hot chocolate.

"Your lips are blue," I said.

"So are yours."

"Here we are," Dad said, holding out a tray with two mugs of steaming chocolate.

I grabbed one and Megan grabbed the other.

"So, what do you girls want to do this afternoon?" Dad asked.

"I'm up for anything…except swimming," Megan said.

"Wimp!" I said.

Megan stuck out her tongue at me, and then we both started giggling again.

"You know," said Megan, "for a snot-nosed, little brat, you're a lot of fun."

"So are you," I said with a grin, "for a cranky teenager who's too cool to move."

"I moved pretty quick when it came time to pull you out of the pool!"

"I really didn't need help," I said.

"Sure you didn't," she said with a nod.

I snuggled up close beside her and watched the fire, counting the stockings that hung on the mantle (one for Dad, one for Mom, one for Megan, and one for me). I slurped some more cocoa and thought how Christmas really is the best time of the year.

The Sirens' Sword

I

Listen. Can you hear them singing? On nights like this, they swim near these shores and raise their haunting voices above the crashing waves. Their melody is mournful, enchanting, some say seductive. They pine for the joys of womanhood--of firelight on the hearth, of a lover's sweet caresses, and babes suckling at the breast-- joys thrust forever beyond their reach by the touch of an enchanted blade.

These sirens, as some name them, were not always denizens of the deep. Each and all were born as mortal maidens. Once, they danced beneath the moon with flowers in their hair, the green grass soft under their tender feet.

But then the Northmen came...

The girl sat with her knees pulled up to her chest, wiggling her pink toes in the warmth of the hearth fire as her grandmother deftly plaited spring flowers into her bright copper hair. She and all the other maidens would be decked in their finest clothes as they gathered to greet the spring equinox with singing and dancing.

Though Grandmother grumbled about the pagan origins of the celebration, she couldn't complain too vehemently since it had been arranged that this year a priest would come from the abbey to bless the crops and the flocks. He would also baptize all the infants born in the past year, perform several marriages and hear confessions and give the sacrament of Holy Communion to everyone who desired it.

While the young woman's mother had been alive, her father, the chieftain, had been faithful to provide a living for a parish priest within their village, but after his wife's burial, he had done away with this "extravagant" expense. Members of his tribe could make the long trek to the abbey, if they desired more religion than he could afford. Or, they could wait for the semi-annual visits from the priests to their village. Too much religion, he felt, did no one any good.

Her grandmother often grumbled about her son-in-law's lack of piety, but she hadn't the means to employ a priest of her own.

"Grandmother, I know the priest will administer all the sacraments when he comes, but what about those who have died? Can he give them a Christian burial, when they've already been laid in the earth?" the girl wondered.

"Christ knows those whose hearts are truly his. Come Resurrection Day, he will gather them all to himself, regardless of the manner in which they've been buried."

"So you don't believe they have to be anointed by a priest and laid in consecrated ground?" It seemed odd to the girl that the pious old woman would think such a thing possible.

"Tell me, Cliona: what ground does not belong to the Lord of all the Earth?" the woman asked, tugging a little too tightly on her granddaughter's flame-colored tresses.

The girl could see the old woman's point, but she was still thankful that her own mother had been given a proper, Christian burial.

"How much longer until the priest arrives?" she wondered.

"He should be here this evening, in time for the feast," the woman answered, tying off the girl's braids with a leather cord. "Now, go and fetch your sister. We've wasted enough time on your vanity. Tell Muirna it's her turn."

Cliona ducked through the low doorway, calling for her sister, who quickly appeared with her arms full of spring wildflowers. Muirna's black locks fell in tangled masses about her face.

"Grandmother is ready for you. Here, take my comb," she said, thrusting it into her sister's hand.

Cliona made her way through the village, waving to her friends. The maidens clustered around her tittering with excitement. Each of them was dressed in her best clothing, yet they all admired Cliona's deep blue dress and the flowers in her hair. It felt good to be beautiful.

The older women of the village smiled and shook their heads, as they shooed them back to their chores. There were cakes to be baked and roasting meat to be tended. So the young women made themselves busy, but all the while they dreamed of the feast to come. There would be singing and dancing and perhaps even handsome young men looking for brides.

Several young couples were planning to have their marriages blessed and solemnized by the priest. Who

knew if some eligible bachelor might decide it was time
to seize this opportunity to wed?

Finally it was time for the great feast to begin. The
board was spread with delicious foods and the golden
mead flowed freely. Yet still, the priest had not come.

When everyone had eaten, the girls got up to
dance. They clasped hands and swayed to the tunes of
the harp and pipe, sometimes whirling about,
sometimes turning in a stately circle, their spirits and
heels made light by the music.

When the music stopped, they clapped with
delight, then stopped to drink and catch their breath.
Cliona looked about for the priest. She went to ask her
grandmother if she had seen him come, but it appeared
that he hadn't arrived yet, though it was getting quite
dark.

The girls gathered once more and by the light of the
rising moon, they formed a solemn circle. They raised
their voices in a sweet, unearthly song as they stepped
lightly over the soft green turf.

"O Lady Mother, bless us
Let our land be bountiful
Let our herds be fruitful
Let our homes be secure
Let your daughters bring forth many strong sons
O Lady Mother, bless us we pray.'

It was an old melody. Though the words were
addressed to the Virgin Mary, the music and its
sentiment had been handed down from a far older
tradition in which the goddess of the earth was invoked
to grant her blessings on the tribe.

For a long time, there was no sound but the song of
the maidens, and the distant crashing of waves on the

beach. Everyone sang along with them in his heart, praying for the blessing that would allow them to live and thrive upon the lands for another year.

Suddenly, their dance was interrupted by a great commotion. Two men astride one donkey charged in among the revelers. Four others raced along behind them on foot, careening into the villagers, and collapsing on the ground. Shouts of protest and alarm arose from all directions.

Cliona's father, the chieftain, stood up and called for silence. "What is the meaning of this?" he demanded.

One of the men dismounted from the donkey and bowed low before the chieftain. "Sanctuary," he croaked.

The men who had run in still lay panting on the ground, unable to catch their breaths.

"Ho there," the chief commanded, pointing to one of the young men of the village. "Fetch these men some water."

The strangers accepted the drink gratefully. The second rider slid down off the donkey, and drank deeply of the water offered to him. Finally, he spoke.

"We are monks from the island abbey. I am Father Dennis, the abbot who was supposed to come here to bless your feast. Before I could depart this morning, our abbey was attacked by a band of savage raiders."

"Raiders?" the chief asked. "Who would dare to attack a monastery?"

Cliona's grandmother spoke up, "They will call the wrath of God down upon themselves."

"They are Vikings. Heathens from the North. They came in their dragon-prowed ships and destroyed everything that they could not steal. My brothers and I were fortunate to escape. We know not whether any others from the abbey have survived."

This news caused no lack of alarm and consternation among the villagers. With their one flank guarded by the river, and the other guarded by the coastline, they had considered themselves well defended against any attackers who came on foot, but enemies who could travel over the waves were another matter. If the abbey, on its remote island, could fall, certainly their little village could be plundered by these brigands.

The festive air of the evening gave way to murmurs of fear. The monks told everything they knew: how the Vikings had hacked down their undefended brethren, how they had stolen articles of gold and silver used by the priests to perform sacred rights, how they had taken illuminated manuscripts decorated with gold from the scriptorium, but then committed all the other documents to the flames.

The more they spoke about the savage Norsemen, the more terrified Cliona became. What if they would not be satisfied with the treasures they had stolen from the monastery? What if they came here next?

Once the monks had concluded their tale, the abbot offered to hear confessions. Apparently, many of the villagers were thinking about the danger which threatened them from the sea-kings, because even the least pious among them were lining up to confess. Better not to face a mortal enemy with your soul's future in doubt.

The Chieftain and his retinue of soldiers talked long into the night, discussing how best to defend their village.

Cliona, Muirna and several of the other maidens clustered around their grandmother.

"What will become of us if the Vikings attack? Will we be carried off and forced to become their wives?" Cliona asked.

"Their slaves, more likely," Muirna grumbled.

"Come, daughters. You must not allow your hearts to be eaten up with fear. We must all fast and pray to our blessed Lord for protection. He will be our shield and defender."

"But if that's so," Cliona wondered, "why didn't he protect the monks?"

In the days that followed, the mood in the village was charged with growing fear. No one spoke of the Norsemen, though every eye watched the coast for their colored sails. The young girls, who used to laugh and sing their way through the days, now clung to one another in terror-stricken silence, ever afraid to be sent out alone.

The old dame urged her son-in-law to call for fasting and prayers among the villagers, but he would not listen. God had failed to defend His own monks; why should He spare their village?

But the chieftain was a man of action. He was not content to sit and wring his hands while waiting for the arrival of the Norsemen. He needed to defend his people, so he resorted to the aid of older gods.

There was an ancient witch woman, who lived alone in a cave near the sea. The chieftain brought her his dilemma.

He returned home from the meeting and ordered his daughters to fill a chest with gold, along with all the jewelry and clothing that had once belonged to their mother.

"Just what do you intend to do with all this?" asked the grandmother.

"I'm buying us safety," the chieftain responded.

"You would take garments fit for a queen and bestow them upon an old hag?"

"If the old hag, as you call her, can give me the advantage I need to defeat my enemies, I would give her all this and more."

"And what will your daughters do for a dowry?"

"When the Norsemen come, they will surely be noble enough to forgo any dowry or blessing from me when they seize my children for their own pleasure. You would have me sit on my hands, but I don't intend to wait around for God to save us. Not when I know the way to defeat our enemies." With that, he shouldered the chest, and returned to the witch.

His mother-in-law just shook her head. "By seeking the aid of witchcraft, he will call down a far worse fate than invasion upon us," she muttered, but no one was listening.

Within a week, the chieftain returned in triumph from his visit to the witch. Cliona's eyes grew wide as her father produced a magnificent sword. Its pommel was shaped like the flukes of a dolphin's tale, and there were strange spells carved into its hilt.

"A single sword. Is that all your offerings have bought you?" the grandmother scoffed.

"Silence, woman. I don't have to listen to your impudent chiding. This is no ordinary sword. It is a magical weapon, which will give us the advantage over our enemies."

"How does it work, father?" Cliona whispered.

"Come along, and I'll show you," the chieftain replied.

He summoned all of his retainers, and every able bodied man to the beach, and before them, he produced the mighty weapon.

"This is an enchanted sword," he proclaimed, "and here is how it works." He sat down upon the sand, and laid the naked blade against his legs with the pommel at his feet. Instantly, his legs were transformed into a fish tail, encased in shimmering scales. The chieftain had become a merrow, one of the mythical mermen who, according to ancient legend, were supposed to lure fishermen to their deaths.

"Once we have transformed ourselves into merrows, we can swim out and meet our enemies before they make landfall. We can tear their boats to splinters and drown them before they can ever reach our shores."

"What happens once we have claimed victory?" one of the men asked. "Will we be trapped in such unnatural forms forever?"

"No," the chief explained. "All we need do is use the magical sword to cut apart our tails, and we will resume the shape of men." Catching up the weapon by its hilts, he deftly sliced apart the glittering fish's tail and his legs were restored.

"What we must do now," the chieftain ordered, "is prepare for battle with the Norsemen. We will meet them on our own terms and fight them to the death."

He set a watch on the coast, so that any sighting of Viking sails would raise an alarm in the village. While they waited, he and his warriors set to work creating

—

weapons with which to fall upon their enemies.

One virtue of the sword's magic was that it allowed them to communicate mind to mind with one another under water. Beneath the waves, they crafted great awl's shaped like stone axe heads, for knocking holes in the Viking's ships. They fashioned sharp, jagged knives of shell with which they could hamstring their enemies and leave their bodies to the sharks. All these special weapons they stored in secret caves under the Merrow Rocks, a rock formation barely visible from the shore where the sirens of the deep supposedly lured the boats of unsuspecting sailors in order to sink them.

Within weeks, the Viking sails were sighted on the horizon, and the alarm rang through the village, "The Norsemen are coming!"

The chieftain and his men raced to the beach, with the magic sword in hand. One by one, they laid it against their legs, then dove into the foaming waves, and swam with all haste out to the Merrow Rocks. Below the water, they circled the Viking ships. At the chieftain's command they began their attack. Within an hour, the stout hulls of the Norse ships had been reduced to splintered flotsam. The mermen wrestled their enemies under the waves, slicing through their hamstrings with stout knives of shell and leaving them to drown. Sharks circled the wreckage, waiting to devour the lifeless bodies of the attackers, while the triumphant chieftain and his entourage swam home.

They were giddy and jubilant as they handed the magical sword from one to the next and slit their tails apart. There was great feasting in the village that night, and the golden mead flowed freely.

The chieftain raised a drinking horn and pledged

his, "Invincible host, and their magic blade."

But there was one person who would not join in the revelry. Cliona took a dish of roasted meat and honey cakes, and went in search of her grandmother. She found her shut up in her cottage, praying.

"Grandmother, I thought you might be hungry..."

"Nay, my child. I will not eat this day. This is a day to mourn and fast, not a day to fill one's belly."

"But, Grandmother, our father and his men have won a great victory. Should we not celebrate the defeat of the Norsemen?"

"Let them gorge themselves until they are sick. This has been no victory except for the forces of darkness."

"What do you mean?" the girl asked.

"They have cheated death by witchcraft, but there are fates far worse than death. Mark my words, this business is not yet at an end. Your father will come to rue the day when he trusted in sorcery to save him."

Cliona left her grandmother alone and went to seek her sister, Muirna. The two of them sat down and began to eat the food which their grandmother had spurned.

"Do you think she is right?" Cliona asked her sister. "Was it so wrong for our father to use the magic sword when it has done all that the witch promised it would? It gave him the strength and cunning to defend our village. If it hadn't been for that sword, we might all be dead."

"Or worse," Muirna said. "Grandmother has many strong opinions, but that doesn't mean she is always right."

Cliona thought about this as she licked the meat

juices off of her fingers. Their father had acted only out of a desire to protect his people. How could that be wrong?

In the weeks that followed, life in the village returned to its former pace. The girls no longer huddled together for fear. The men and women of the village felt safe and content. The chieftain set a continual watch on the seacoast, soldiers who could swiftly raise the alarm, should any Viking sails appear on the horizon. Only the grandmother went through her days muttering about the woe that would surely come upon them because they had put their trust in witchcraft.

The chief would listen to none of her reproof. "If you are so certain that we are doomed to disaster, why don't you leave?" he said. "Go find yourself an abbey where you can mutter your prayers and light your candles in the company of other Christians as devout as yourself. I'm tired of listening to your dire auguries."

From that day on, the grandmother avoided discussing her forebodings with her son-in-law. She kept out of his way as much as possible, and would only speak to him when she was first spoken to.

Weeks drew on into months, and it seemed that Heaven smiled upon them. The flocks were healthy, the crops gave every promise of being bountiful, and the dreaded Norsemen were nowhere to be seen. So it came as a shock the morning Cliona heard commotion in the village. The stench of burning thatch smote her nostrils. Something was horribly wrong.

Her sister, Muirna, came running from the riverbank, with a group of maidens at her heels. "The Vikings are coming!" she screamed.

"But the watchmen gave no warning."

"They sailed up the river, and have already made landfall."

What would they do? The girls had nowhere to go. They would surely be captured, and raped. Killed or enslaved. They had to escape, but how?

Cliona ran for her father's hall, where the great magic sword was kept. She took it up and ran back to the maidens, crying, "Follow me!"

They ran with all haste to the beach, and there on the sand, Cliona laid the blade against her white legs. Instantly, they were transformed into a mermaid's tail.

"Quickly!" she called to the others, as she dragged herself into the surf. She swam up and down near the shore, encouraging the others to use the sword.

One by one, they took their turns, until all had been transformed into mermaids. Just as the last maiden was diving into the surf, the Viking host came charging down from the village. Their captain seized the magic blade which lay abandoned on the strand, and raised it aloft, waving it at the helpless girls in mockery. They had escaped from the Vikings, but now their enemies held the only means they had of returning safely from the sea. Their fear had driven them to what had seemed a place of safety, but they would be forever trapped there as a consequence...

For many hundred years now they have roamed the pathless oceans with no way to come home, no one to slice through the scaly bonds which hold them captive in freakish bodies which are neither wholly woman nor fully fish.

Somewhere beneath the island's emerald sod, their

dread enemy, the great sea king, now sleeps in his high-prowed ship with an enchanted sword at his feet, while the sirens, with their silvery tails and fair white breasts--round and firm and useless--cry out for their lost womanhood and the repose they can never know.

Perhaps you are the one they call for--the one who will find the ancient sword and restore their humanity, or else help them to eternal peace at last. For, indeed, there are some fates worse than death.

II

It was John's overdeveloped sense of chivalry that always seemed to get him into trouble where Cynthia was concerned. He no longer harbored any illusions regarding how she felt about him personally. In her eyes, he had long ago been, "weighed in the balance and found wanting." She was like too many other smart, sophisticated women whom he'd tried, and failed to impress.

As he stood on the front steps of the history museum, clad in his tuxedo and tight shoes, he wondered for the thousandth time just why he'd let Cynthia's brother, Bryan, talk him into making an appearance at the gala reception which they were throwing to celebrate the long-awaited opening of her Viking Ship Burial exhibit. Tonight, he would pose as the distinguished archeologist's inconspicuous beau, or, as he was sure Cynthia would probably introduce him, her "very dear friend, John." It was all a great pretense, a fraud.

Cynthia had no interest in a romantic relationship, yet there were times (like this evening, or at Bryan's numerous wedding receptions) when she seemed to find being alone awkward. On such occasions she was not above recruiting John as her impromptu escort. It was simply easier to already have a designated dance partner, and so she had been content to let John fill the bill.

Nothing was more precious to Cynthia than her academic career. John saw her as a type of Rapunzel who, having cut off her own hair, now found herself trapped in an ivory tower. For his part, he felt somehow compelled to come to the aid of this damsel in distress, even though he recognized the distress was of her own making.

He pushed open the museum's great, glass door, and looked about the large foyer. The gleaming, soft grey marble of the floor echoed under his feet as he walked toward the coat room on his left. This great hall was rarely so quiet. It was usually crowded with gangs of school children, in rumpled uniforms, who couldn't quite stand still in their straight lines, and tour groups of vacationers, clad in shorts with cameras in their hands, speaking to each other in foreign tongues.

Though the museum was unusually empty, its distinctive smell was just the same as John had remembered it. The air here always smelled too clean. It wasn't an antiseptic smell, instead it smelled like air that had been carefully purified and humidity controlled; distilled air that had had all the natural and human elements stripped away. There was no taint of pollen or earth, of sweat or blood.

In a way John thought it ironic, considering the fact that most of the items which were so carefully housed here had been dug out of graves and garbage dumps. One tended to forget when walking through the museum that these "artifacts" were the detritus of real human lives. They had been fashioned and handled by real men and women who had been forced to discard them only because they themselves had lain down and died.

A ghostly chill ran down John's spine. In the sepulchral silence of the empty museum, he found such thoughts unnerving. His footsteps resounded through the vast space, as he hurried to the cloak room entrance where a young woman, uniformed in a tired blue blazer, scrutinized the guest list on her clip board. She directed him around the corner, and then to the third gallery on the right.

He stood for a moment with one hand poised on the heavy, paneled door, as he wiped a damp palm against his trouser leg before making his entrance. Stepping through the door was like entering another world. The bright hum of a dozen witty conversations flooded over him. The gallery was well lit and bedecked here and there with festive floral arrangements. At the far end of the gallery, a second pair of heavy, paneled, double doors mirrored the ones he had just come through. Grey-haired gentlemen in tuxedos, and stately older women encrusted with jewels stood chatting in small clusters. White-gloved waiters circulated among the guests with trays of hors d' oeuvres and champagne. They flitted from group to group like bees busily pollinating a meadow of colorful flowers.

John began making his way around the outskirts of the room, scanning the faces for any he might find familiar.

"There you are. I've been looking for you everywhere." John turned to see Bryan coming toward him, carrying a half-empty glass of champagne.

"Cynthia will be thrilled to see you. She was laying odds that you'd come up with a last minute excuse, and scarper," Bryan continued. "But I stood up for you. Come on, I'll take you to her."

Bryan grabbed John by the elbow and maneuvered him in and out among the clusters of chatting guests. He flagged down a waiter with a tray of champagne glasses. Tossing off what remained of his drink in a single gulp, he exchanged his empty glass for two full ones. "Here, have some champagne," he said, handing one to John.

Soon they approached the corner where Cynthia was holding court. She was surrounded by a sizable gathering, all of whom were extolling her work. As far as John could see, she was positively eating it up. He edged his way into the circle, and caught Cynthia's eye. She immediately turned her attention to him.

"John! How wonderful to see you. I'm so glad you could make it." She warmly extended her hand to him, slightly inclining her head in his direction. John recognized his cue.

"Hello, Cynthia. You look lovely," he said. He obligingly kissed her on the cheek as he took her hand. He knew his part, and he would play it well.

Cynthia really did look lovely. If he hadn't known her so well, he might have even found her attractive. She wore an evening dress of midnight blue silk, with a scarf of the same color wrapped about her and pinned on one shoulder with a replica of a Viking brooch. A long pin secured the fabric, passing in and out through an intricately decorated open ring. Her shoulder length brown hair had been painstakingly styled, and her glasses had disappeared, in favor of contact lenses, though the tell-tale red lines radiating from the blue of her eyes betrayed the fact that she was unaccustomed to wearing them.

"Let me introduce you," Cynthia said taking his arm. "This is Dr. Raeburn, the head of my department at the university, and his wife Elaine," she said, gesturing to the couple on her right. "And this," she said, referring to himself, "is my very dear friend,

John."

Dr. Raeburn shot him a knowing smile and John congratulated himself on the believability of his performance. The professor shook his hand vigorously.

"You must be very proud of Cynthia, here," he said with a smile. "Of course, we all are. Why, I was just saying to Elaine the other day, 'That girl has outdone herself.'"

Only John appeared to have noticed the scowl which flashed across Cynthia's countenance at his use of the term "girl."

The professor went on, "She's made her mark with this one. From now on she'll be one of the best recognized names in archeology."

Cynthia smiled modestly. "Just call me 'Indiana Jones,'" she said, taking a sip of her champagne.

"I'm serious," Dr. Raeburn continued. "This Viking Ship Burial is your magnum opus, your master work. I don't know how you'll ever be able to top this one."

The man's tone was jovial, but John was unsure if this was meant as a compliment or a veiled threat. He glanced at Cynthia. For a moment, the look in her eyes reminded him of a cornered animal. It was obvious to him that she found the idea of having nothing further to achieve a threatening prospect.

John felt he ought to say something to diffuse the tension. He had hoped that this evening's performance would be primarily a walk-on part.

"I'm certainly looking forward to seeing the exhibit," he offered. It wasn't much help, but Cynthia seemed to relax a little. She wasn't smiling, but she didn't look quite so unnerved.

Just then, a small man with the air of a stage

manager sidled up to her and discreetly said, "Pardon me, Dr. Hengist, but we'd like to get started, whenever you're ready."

"Of course, Mr. Devers. Thank you," she responded. Turning to the group at large, she said, "If you'll excuse me, I need to go and make sure that everything is in order for my presentation."

She followed Devers out one of the large doors at the far end of the room, while the crowd which had flocked about her scattered in various directions.

John found himself suddenly standing all alone. He glanced around for Bryan. It wasn't long before he spotted him. He appeared to be deeply engrossed in a conversation with a young woman who looked to be half Bryan's age. John guessed she was probably one of Cynthia's graduate assistants. She was wearing a low-cut halter dress, covered with swirling designs of turquoise and violet. Her hair, which had obviously been dyed in streaks of red and gold, was piled in a twist at the back of her head. A bronze arm ring coiled above her right elbow like a serpent, and a diamond twinkled in her left nostril. An ornate pentangle adorned her neck.

The young woman apparently found Bryan fascinating. She was hanging on his every word. *There's no accounting for Bryan's magnetism.* John thought, with a touch of envy. *Some have it, some don't.*

Bryan paused for a moment to introduce her. "John, this is Hillary Swanson. She helped Cynthia dig all this stuff up. Hillary, this is John. He's Cynthia's paramour de jure."

"Oh," said Hillary, clearly surprised. "Delighted to meet you! How long have you and Dr. Hengist been together?"

John cleared his throat. "We're not exactly together...," he began.

"No. John's just an old friend of the family who's here to help Cynthia prop up the illusion that she has a social life," Bryan said. "Apparently, the obsessive, celibate, academic 'shoe' was *not* the one she wanted to wear on this occasion, even though it fits her so well."

Hillary burst out laughing.

John chuckled politely, while silently giving thanks that champagne was the only thing being served. Who knew what Bryan might say after a couple of pints of stout?

At that moment, both the great doors at the end of the room were thrown wide open. Mr. Devers stood in the doorway for a moment, surveying the crowd.

"May I have your attention, please? If you could all come this way, Dr. Hengist will begin her lecture in five minutes."

John moved through the open doors into the adjoining gallery and found a seat near the back, as Mr. Devers stepped up to the podium. "It is my very great pleasure," he began, "to introduce Dr. Cynthia Hengist."

The audience applauded as Cynthia took her place at the lectern.

"The early Vikings buried great stores of treasure along with their most distinguished leaders," she began. "All that an eorl, or nobleman, might need in the afterlife would be buried along with him in a great ship, which they believed could sail him to the next world. This particular ship burial dates back to the mid-800's, only a few years after the Viking conquest of the monastery at Lindisfarne."

Cynthia went on to show slides featuring the excavation site, along with artifacts which had been unearthed. She explained that the person buried here had been a great Viking war leader, and many of the objects which she and her team had recovered were the products of other cultures, obtained either through trade, or conquest. After a few more slides which showed some of the process involved in preserving the artifacts, she concluded her remarks, and invited everyone to enjoy touring the actual exhibit.

Mr. Devers handed her a large set of scissors and asked her to cut the red ribbon strung across the doorway, which she did, to the accompaniment of enthusiastic applause.

John waited for the majority of the guests to file through the doors, then tagged along behind. Most of the people hurried through, taking only a few minutes to file past display cases filled with exquisite Norse armor, shields, blades, brooches and golden torques, all of which had been buried along with the Viking lord. John's approach was more thorough. He took his time and really examined the pieces, reading the display boards which accompanied them. It was all beautiful and extraordinary. He could well believe that this was Cynthia's magnum opus.

He turned the corner into one of the final galleries and stood stock still in amazement. There, bathed in silver light, hung the most incredible sword he had ever seen suspended from the ceiling. It was long and smooth and gleaming, without the telltale notches and divots which hard use in battle usually left behind, or the pock-marks which marred the surfaces of the other metal objects which had spent hundreds of years buried beneath the earth. It was so well preserved that it might have been forged yesterday.

John stared at the artifact, transfixed by its beauty. He noticed that there were what appeared to be Celtic runes graven into the hilt. The pommel was oddly shaped, like the cloven flukes of a dolphin's tail. He reached his hand toward it, trying to imagine, just for a moment, what it might feel like to wield such a weapon. Quickly he let his hand drop back to his side, glancing around to see if anyone near had witnessed his faux pas. Any school boy would know better than to even imagine touching such a thing. After all, this was a museum, not a toyshop.

"It is breathtaking, isn't it?"

John turned to see Cynthia standing just a little behind him.

"What was it used for?"

"That's the really sad part. We don't know." Her air was apologetic. "I was a little reluctant when I found out they wanted to feature this piece so prominently in the display. Out of everything we unearthed, this is probably the artifact that I know the least about, but it was so well preserved that I couldn't deny them."

"I noticed the runes there on the hilt. What do they say?"

"It's an ancient tongue related to Gaelic, but nobody I've tried to contact has been able to decipher it. Our supposition is that this was a ceremonial sword…"

"Which would explain why it has been preserved in such pristine condition."

"Yes, and the writing may be some kind of arcane incantation, known only to an initiated elite of druids or magicians."

John raised an eyebrow, but said nothing.

Just then Bryan stepped up, accompanied by Cynthia's graduate assistant, Hillary.

"Hi, John. Hi, Cyn. Hillary, here, says I just have to see the magic sword."

Hillary ignored both John and Cynthia, and pointed at the sword, dragging Bryan toward it with her other arm. "You see? Didn't I tell you it was incredible?"

Bryan gave a low whistle and nodded appreciatively. "I've never seen anything like it."

"It's enchanted," Hillary went on. "Those markings on the hilt are spells...and listen." She motioned for silence. "Do you hear that humming? That vibration is part of the magic."

Cynthia scowled. She clearly objected to Hillary proclaiming her superstitions as if they were verifiable facts.

"So if it's a magic sword, what's it supposed to do?" Bryan asked.

"Whatever its makers intended it to do, it could not save them from the Vikings," Cynthia chimed in with an authoritative tone. "Our Viking chieftain obviously thought it a great prize, or his people wouldn't have bothered to bury it at their lord's feet. Whatever it represented to the people who made it, to the Norsemen it represented their triumph."

"Well, I have to say that this entire exhibit represents your triumph," John said. "You've done incredible work here and you have every right to be proud."

Cynthia glanced away, both gratified and embarrassed.

"You tell her, John." Bryan chimed in. "This exhibit is her baby, and even though it's only just opened, she's been moping about for days with a terrible case of post-partum depression. Her name's about to become a household word, and she's already worried about becoming a has-been."

"I'm just a bit nervous about what comes next," Cynthia retorted. "Where do I go from here?"

"I'd guess you take the exhibit on tour," John offered.

"Yes, of course, if I'm fortunate enough to find the sponsors. But that's not what I'm talking about."

"She'll never admit it, but she's a driven workaholic who simply doesn't know how to enjoy her own success," said Bryan.

Cynthia shot her brother a black look. "It's not that. It's just that I've been working on this for so long..."

"You'll make another even greater discovery," John reassured her.

"That's right," Hillary chimed in. "Either you'll find the work, or it will find you. It's your destiny."

"Perhaps you're right," Cynthia said, with a tentative smile.

Hillary turned to Bryan. "Come on," she said, dragging him by the hand "you have to see the rest of the exhibit."

Once they had gone, Cynthia turned back to John. "You'll have to excuse my research assistant. Hillary fancies herself something of a neo-pagan. She tends to blur the distinction between ancient legend and historical fact."

With a knowing smile, John quoted *Hamlet*, "There are more things in heaven and earth, Horatio, than are dreamt of in your philosophy."

Cynthia frowned, clearly distressed by his implication that she, the professional archeologist, might be somehow closed-minded for dismissing Hillary's superstitions.

"Do you wonder a great deal about the people whose odds and ends you dig up?" John asked.

"Well, of course I wonder about their lifestyles, their culture, their habits. Every artifact is like a puzzle piece that we gradually fit together to get a picture of what their daily lives were like."

"Yes, but I was thinking more of the individuals. The man who carried that sword, for example. What was his name? If he could speak to us from the high and far off past, what story would he tell?"

"Those kinds of questions are better left to poets and philosophers," she responded. "I, myself, am merely a scientist."

Just then, a bevy of well dressed, older men and women swarmed into the room, surrounding Cynthia and expressing their admiration for the fantastic sword in glowing terms. These were the wealthy patrons whom Cynthia needed to impress. If she played her cards right, they had the potential to send her exhibit on a world tour. She turned her full attention to them, and was soon caught up in a detailed discussion. Recognizing this as the proper cue for his exit, John slipped quietly around the corner into the next gallery.

There were several more displays, but none so striking as the sword. During the drive home, John couldn't stop thinking about it. It haunted him like an image from a dream. He wondered about the people who had crafted it. Who were they, and what had they hoped it could do for them? There were so many questions that even Cynthia couldn't yet answer. He wondered if they would remain unanswered forever. Somehow, the thought made him feel very sad.

That weekend, John decided to go sailing. For John, sailing was far more than a pastime. It was his passion. He had loved boats ever since he was a little boy, and had always dreamed of owning one.

When, at the age of forty-six, he had looked around and realized that he would probably never have a wife to support or children to put through school, he'd decided to take all of his savings and buy a boat of his own. It was a move which Bryan had deemed completely out of character for the retiring literature professor.

John didn't usually stay out on the water after dark, but this evening he had packed a picnic supper and headed out, not intending to come back until much later.

He felt the need to clear his head, and sailing was always the best way for him to do that. The sea was fairly quiet, the waves gentle. He was enjoying the profound stillness which was broken only by the occasional crying of gulls and the soft sounds of water lapping against his boat.

He strained his ears to listen to the stillness, trying to open his soul to it.

The sun set and the full moon rose, a pale, white giant against the horizon. All the while, John kept perfectly silent, trying to allow the quiet to envelope him. It was then that he first heard the voices. He looked around to see if there was someone in trouble.

The sounds seemed to be coming from the Merrow Rocks, a large rock formation barely within sight of shore. According to local legend, the merpeople (or merrows) would sit upon those rocks, singing their sirens' songs to lure fishermen to their deaths.

John didn't give the legends much credence, but he did wonder whether perhaps a small boat had run aground on the rocks. That might be the source of the cries.

He turned the tiller and made for the Merrow Rocks. Though the moon was very bright, it was hard to see much at this distance. He fetched a pair of binoculars and scanned the rocks for any sign of wreckage.

"Perhaps the vocalizations aren't human at all. Maybe they're seals, or something," he thought, but the voices grew louder as he approached.

Soon, their lament took on a more melodic tone, as if many voices were singing a sad song all together. John was unable to distinguish the words, but the music was heartbreaking.

Common sense told him that he needed to turn about, but he felt compelled to find the singers, whoever they might be, and to help them if he could.

Soon, he was close enough that he could make out figures poised upon the rocks when he looked through his binoculars, but what they were was too difficult to tell. Just at the point where he knew he must not come any closer, he realized that the great chorus of sad and desperate singers was moving in his direction. The creatures began to circle his boat at a distance, slowly drawing nearer and nearer as their song grew in volume and intensity.

John peered at them in the pale moonlight. There could be no mistake now that they were so close. Their upper bodies were those of women, while their hindquarters resembled the tails of great fish, but with flat flukes, like those of a whale or dolphin. They were mermaids, sirens who had come to lure him to the rocks and sink his boat.

He knew his position was perilous, yet somehow he didn't feel any panic. "What do you want of me?" he cried out. "You have called me, and I have come. Now what must I do?"

A copper-haired mermaid swam close to his boat, reaching up for the side. Her preternatural beauty was marred only by the grief in her countenance. John leaned down to her to hear what she might tell him.

She stretched upward and grasped his hand. No sooner had she done so, than pictures began forming in John's mind. It was like nothing he had ever experienced before. Somehow, through the touch of her mind the mermaid was communicating their strange and sorrow-filled history.

He could picture them as young girls, dancing in the moonlight. Then he saw the terrified monks who had fled from the ruin of their monastery. Through the girl's eyes he saw the consternation of the chieftain, and the warnings of her grandmother. He could see the enchanted sword, and the success it brought the men in battle against the Norsemen, and then the horror of the Vikings' secret attack up the river, of the girls fleeing for their lives and using the magic blade to escape into the ocean, only to have the means of breaking the enchantment thrust forever out of their reach.

The days had grown into years, which had grown into decades, which had grown into centuries, and still the pathetic creatures remained trapped, doomed to wander the pathless oceans in eternal exile. Now and again, they would swim back to the shores that had once been their homeland, and come to the Merrow Rocks to mourn for all they had lost.

The mermaids' history was heartbreaking. John was practically in tears as the one who called herself Cliona revealed the many long years during which they had been exiled from land. To be cut off from humanity … to have their lives unnaturally drawn out by the strength of the enchantment that held them captive. The weariness of a thousand lifetimes of sorrow flowed from the mermaid's mind into his heart. He could well believe that theirs was a fate worse than death, just as their grandmother had warned.

From the pictures in his mind, John at once recognized the magic sword as the one which was housed in the ship burial exhibit.

"I have seen the sword you seek," he said aloud. Grasping tightly to the mermaid's hand, he closed his eyes and pictured it in his mind.

The copper-haired mermaid grew very excited. "You bring to us? You set us free?" she begged in the best semblance of English she could glean from John's mind.

John pondered just how he could he get his hands on the sword. In the museum, it was carefully guarded, and besides, John was no thief. Yet, would giving the sword to these poor creatures really be stealing? After all, the old witch had made it for their tribe in the first place. Weren't they really its rightful owners? The Viking king had taken it as a spoil of his conquest, and then Cynthia had come along and robbed his grave. From that point of view, John would really be doing the right thing by returning the sword to them.

He looked at the poor mermaids, their hair hanging limp over their shoulders. Their eyes were so forlorn, and their story was so desperately sad. All they wanted was freedom — release from the enchantment which had imprisoned them for generations.

"I will do what I can to get the sword," he promised. "Then you can be free of your banishment and find the peace you seek."

Cliona seemed deeply moved by his words. Grasping his hand tightly in her own, she brought it to her lips and kissed it, weeping for joy.

With that, the mermaids resumed their mournful song, slowly circling John's boat. Then one by one, they dove beneath the waves and disappeared from sight. There was nothing but the gentle slap of waves against the boat and the great, pale moon shining down on the water. John wondered if the strange incident had all been a dream.

The mermaid's heartbreaking tale and grateful tears had won him over. This damsel in distress was depending on him, as no woman had ever depended upon him before. He determined in his heart that, come what may, he must not fail her. He turned his boat back toward the dock, all the while humming the mermaid's soft lament.

Later that week, John stopped by Cynthia's office to talk with her about the sword. He had to convince her to let him take it, but she would never believe the real reason he needed it, so he struggled to come up with some viable excuse for removing the blade from the museum.

When he arrived, he found that Hillary Swanson was the only person in the office.

"May I help you?" the graduate assistant asked

John debated just what he should say. "It's about the sword, from the Viking exhibit at the museum. You remember you said it was enchanted?"

"Yes."

"Well, I think I have found a local expert in ancient pagan practices who might be able to decipher the markings on the hilt and to reveal what the sword was intended for."

"Really?" Hillary sounded more excited than dubious.

"The problem is I would have to bring the blade to her so that she could examine it personally."

Hillary frowned. "Why can't she come down to the museum?"

"She's very old and infirm," John began, reaching for any excuse. "And she's something of an agoraphobe—doesn't go out in public, you know."

"Look, John, I'm sorry, but this is highly irregular. That sword is a priceless artifact."

"It's more than priceless, Hillary. I don't think Dr. Hengist really understands the occultic powers invested in that blade. It could be very dangerous if handled flippantly."

Hillary looked pensive. John suspected that her own belief in pagan ritual magic set her at odds with her superior's more conventional and scientific outlook on such things. If he could win Hillary over, he might not have to take his outrageous request directly to Cynthia.

"Dr. Hengist would never see herself in such a light, but from the perspective of the druid or wiccan who fashioned that sword, she is little better than a grave robber," John went on. "If my expert can decipher the spells upon the sword, perhaps they will reveal a way to ward off any curse Dr. Hengist might have brought down upon herself by meddling with it."

Hillary sighed heavily. "Look, I'll see if I can't get it taken off exhibit and brought in to the office. I'll tell them it needs further cleaning, or something. But I doubt that Dr. Hengist would approve your taking it away without her personal supervision."

"Well," John responded, "do whatever you can."

*****

"Magic expert?" Cynthia frowned as her assistant related all the details of her strange conversation with John.

"He said she was a local expert in ancient pagan practices."

"And she absolutely can't come examine it in the museum?"

"No. John insisted that he would have to take the sword to her."

There was something fishy going on here. Cynthia determined that she needed more information, and she knew just who could get it for her.

Last month, when her brother Bryan's third wife had kicked him out of the house for good, he had come crawling to Cynthia's doorstep. She had been magnanimously allowing him to stay in her home ever since, so he certainly owed her something. That evening when he walked through the door, she pounced.

"Bryan, I need you to take John out to lunch."

The next evening, following their meeting, Cynthia interrogated Bryan about how it had gone.

"Frankly, I'm worried about John," Bryan responded. "First he told me he was going into a life of crime stealing precious artifacts and selling them on the black market. When I told him to be serious, he came up with the most outrageous cock and bull story about finding mermaids. I think he may be cracking up."

"Mermaids?"

"Yes. He says they came to him out by the Merrow Rocks and that they are looking for the sword from your exhibit. According to John, they are trapped under a spell which can only be broken by that sword. I think he's lost it."

Cynthia didn't say anything. She might not admit to a belief in witchcraft, but she'd been an archeologist long enough to know that old legends, like those surrounding the Merrow Rocks, usually have at least some connection to human history.

It wasn't like John to lie, and it wasn't like him to make up such a fanciful story. Something had motivated him to ask for the sword. She wanted to see for herself just what it was.

She put in a call to Allen, the helicopter pilot with whom she had worked on the Viking Burial. He had flown them over the sight to take aerial photographs of the mound before she and her colleagues began excavating, and then he had made several other flights which allowed them to document the progress of the diggings.

"Hello, Allen? This is Cynthia Hengist," she began. "Listen, I was wondering if you might be available to take me up to get some overhead shots of the Merrow Rocks."

"Sure, Doc. Whatever you need."

The next day, she drove out to the private airstrip where she had booked the helicopter, laden with photographic equipment and video cameras. The morning was clear and a stiff breeze was blowing.

"So, just what are we looking for, Doc?" Allen asked, as he helped Cynthia aboard the helicopter.

"I'm not exactly sure…" she replied, strapping herself in and arranging her camera equipment. "I'm hoping I'll know it when I see it."

They took off, and flew directly out over the ocean. The water was choppy, but they could see a few boats and the occasional spray from a dolphin. It was high tide as they approached the Merrow Rocks, and the formations were all but hidden under the waves. Cynthia began snapping photos, but there was really nothing unusual to be seen.

"Can you come down and circle them lower?" she asked

Allen nodded. Cynthia pulled out her video camera, as the helicopter spiraled downward. They circled the rock formation three times, while she was filming, but nothing remarkable appeared.

"I guess that's it," she said.

Allen pulled back on the stick and the helicopter started to climb. That was when Cynthia caught a glimpse of white faces, just breaking the surface of the water. There were three of them, ghostly pale, each wearing a haunted expression.

"Wait!" she shouted, pulling out her camera. "Go back!"

Cynthia began shooting pictures as fast as she could. As they dropped lower, the creatures dove under the water, and Cynthia caught a clear glimpse of one silvery green tail covered in shimmering fish scales.

"Was that what I think it was?" Allen asked.

Cynthia nodded, still snapping pictures. "It very well might be," she whispered. She sat in stunned silence as Allen turned the helicopter back toward land. John had been telling the truth, after all.

When she got back to the office, Cynthia downloaded her camera onto her computer. The images were hazy at best, but when she blew them up and enhanced them, the startling pictures of human-like faces, and a fish-like tail became more obvious.

Fuzzy photographs of alleged mermaids could get Cynthia noticed in a tabloid or two, but she wanted more. If she could capture one of the creatures, it would be the find of the century in marine biology. She began to scheme her approach. She'd take as small a crew as possible, armed with nets and tranquilizer guns. They would need to capture just one of the creatures and get it back to land, where she could study it. The very idea sent shivers of excitement running down her spine. If the Viking ship burial had put her on the map, this could catapult her to stardom.

*****

John hadn't mentioned it to Bryan, but he had been taking his boat out to visit the mermaids every chance he got. He wanted them to know that he hadn't abandoned them. In spite of what might seem a lack of progress, he had every intention of following through with his promise to bring them the sword, if he could only figure out how to get his hands on it.

But there was more to his visits than merely a desire to reassure the mermaids. He was falling in love with Cliona. More than anything, he did not want to let her down. Here was a woman who did not scorn him, as so many others had. She welcomed his visits. She wanted and needed him.

The next time he came out to the Merrow Rocks, she swam out to meet his boat.

"John," she cried, "there is much danger."

"Why?"

Reaching up for his hand, she closed her eyes and pictured a helicopter circling the rocks. "We must leave very soon or be caught!"

John didn't know how he could bear to lose her. "Please, just wait a little longer. I will bring you the sword as soon as I can," he promised. He admitted to himself that he'd been stalling, unwilling to take the risk of stealing the sword. But they were all running out of time. And he had a pretty good idea of who might have been spying on the mermaids.

That evening, he went directly to Cynthia's house and knocked at the door.

"John! Come in and sit down," she said.

John stepped inside but remained standing. "Look, Cynthia, I'm not sure what you're planning, but I'm asking you to think again…"

"What are you talking about?"

"Someone took a helicopter out over the Merrow Rocks to spy on the mermaids. That was your doing, wasn't it?"

Cynthia stared John straight in the eye. She neither confirmed nor denied his accusation.

"I've known you too long not to suspect that you've got something up your sleeve. I'm sure that to you these creatures represent a great career opportunity. You could be the scientist who finally proves the existence of one of mankind's most persistent myths."

"I don't know what you are talking about."

"The hell you don't!" John burst out. He fought to regain control of himself before going on, "Please consider, you have the opportunity, for once in your life, to think about the needs of others, instead of just your own. I'm begging you, Cynthia, help them. Give them the sword so that they can break the spell and be free."

"That sword is a priceless artifact. I have no intention..."

John cut her off before she could finish. "You use people, Cynthia. You've used me again and again, and now you want to use these poor mermaids to make your name great. It's wrong and it's cruel."

Cynthia's face blanched and she staggered backward a step. Quickly recovering, she proclaimed, "I don't need to stand here and listen to your insults, John." She pulled the door open with a dramatic flourish. "I think it's time for you to go."

John shook his head. "You're heartless. You know that?"

"I'm a scientist," Cynthia replied. "It's my job." With that, she slammed the door behind him.

*****

Cynthia's cheeks burned as she collapsed into a

chair. How dare John accuse her of using him? With an irrational flush of jealousy, she realized that she no longer held the man in thrall. Whatever unrequited, courtly attachment he might have harbored for her had been supplanted by his newly kindled passion for the mermaids. She felt her throat tighten as she brushed away an angry tear.

Grabbing the telephone, she hastily dialed the museum. "Hello, Mr. Devers? This is Dr. Cynthia Hengist. I'd like to discuss beefing up the security on the sword in the Viking exhibit."

"I can assure you that the entire exhibit is being carefully guarded," Devers replied.

"Yes, but I have reason to believe that there may be a plot to steal that sword. I know you wouldn't want anything like that to happen."

"No! Of course not."

"Then, I think that the wisest course would be to take it off exhibit for a couple of weeks while I investigate the rumors further."

"Certainly, Dr. Hengist. We can move it to the museum's vault until you think it's safe to put it back on display."

Cynthia smiled. "Thank you, Mr. Devers. I knew I could count on you."

*****

John arrived at the museum an hour and a half before closing time. He wandered through the echoing galleries, looking for fire exits, any way to get quickly out of the building.

When the museum closed, he hid behind a trash receptacle instead of making his way back to the main entrance. He held his breath and froze in place as a security guard made a tour of the area. As soon as the man was gone, John ducked through the entrance to the Viking burial exhibit. Moving as silently as a cat, he stole around the corner and looked up to see only empty space where the sword had once hung. A small sign on the barricade surrounding the area read, "Artifacts temporarily off display for restoration."

Might Hillary have actually followed up on her promise to have the piece taken out of the exhibit so that his "witchcraft expert" could examine it? Or was Cynthia behind the sword's disappearance? It seemed probable that Cynthia, having refused to help the mermaids herself, might take action to hinder anybody else from coming to their aid.

John snuck out of the museum, debating what his next move ought to be. He stopped at a chemist's shop on the way home and picked up a bottle of chloroform.

The following morning dawned gray and blustery, with ominous clouds threatening a major storm. Even indoors, the wind whistling down the chimney flue made it hard for John to hear as he telephoned Hillary.

"I saw that the sword is off exhibit," he began, raising his voice above the violence of the wind.

"What?" she asked in alarm.

"Didn't you get permission to take it out of the museum?"

"No! I haven't heard anything about this."

"Perhaps it would be best if we looked into it," John suggested. "If the sword really is cursed, Dr. Hengist doesn't have the sense to recognize its power. Each passing day could mean deeper danger. Something must be done before anyone is seriously hurt."

"You're right. I'll meet you at the museum in one hour."

"Drive carefully," John warned. "The weather looks pretty bleak." John grabbed an umbrella and a heavy overcoat. He slipped a handkerchief and the chloroform into its pocket.

Once Hillary arrived at the museum, she marched up to the front desk and demanded to see Mr. Devers, the curator.

"What's going on with the Celtic sword from the Viking exhibit? I heard that you've taken it off display."

"That's right. Dr. Hengist requested that we remove it for safe keeping. I can assure you, the sword is completely secure."

"I'll be the judge of that. I'm Hillary Swanson, Dr. Hengist's research assistant. "

"Oh, Ms. Swanson. We met at the reception."

"Yes, that's right. Now, show me what you've done with the sword."

"If you'll just follow me," Devers said. He led them through a series of deserted corridors, then down a steep stairway to a large metal safe door. "This is the vault," he explained, as he entered the combination and turned the wheel to open the door. "We keep all the pieces of our permanent collection here when they are not on display." He led them through a maze of wooden boxes in various shapes and sizes, until they came to a long, narrow crate.

As he began working to pry open the box lid, John stole up behind Hillary with a chloroform soaked handkerchief in his hand. Making sure that Devers was not looking in his direction, he silently clapped the handkerchief over her mouth and nose, holding it firmly in place until she collapsed in his arms. He laid her on the floor and then cried out in alarm, "I think she's having a stroke!"

Devers turned around to see the young woman lying limp on the floor.

John made a show of feeling for her carotid artery. "She hasn't got a pulse! Go get help!" he ordered.

Devers wavered for a moment, unsure of what to do.

"I told you to go get help!" John yelled. "You don't want her to die, do you?"

Swiftly, Devers turned and ran out the vault door, while John pretended to begin CPR. As soon as the curator was gone, he pried the crate lid free, pulled out the sword, and then swiftly wrapped it in his overcoat. With a last look at the unconscious young woman, he whispered, "I'm really sorry, Hillary," then raced out of the vault, up the stairs, and out the nearest fire exit.

The rain was falling in sheets as he left the museum. Crashes of thunder nearly drowned out the siren wails of arriving emergency vehicles, as he started up his car. He had done what he promised. It was the first time in his life that he remembered doing anything quite so bold and courageous, and it felt good. He was still a little nervous about what the repercussions would be when they discovered the sword was missing, but right now he could only think about poor Cliona and her sisters.

John drove to the harbor, intending to waste no time in getting the sword to the mermaids, but the violence of the storm gave him pause. Waves the height of rooftops were crashing in upon the shore. There was no way that he could take his small boat out in weather like this. Yet he had made a solemn promise to the woman he loved that he would rescue her from her horrible plight. He couldn't falter now.

He parked at the marina, as close to where his boat was docked as he dared to go and sat in silence watching the sheets of driving rain hurl themselves against his windshield. The enchanted sword, still wrapped in his overcoat, lay across his lap. At the first sign that the storm was abating, he intended to dash to his boat and take to the water. Then the world-weary mermaid would find rest at last.

*****

After asking Devers to take the sword off exhibit, Cynthia had wasted no time in chartering a research boat and assembling a crew to go out to the Merrow Rocks. She gathered from what John had told her that her helicopter flight had already disturbed the mermaids. If she intended to capture one of the creatures alive, she knew she needed to act quickly, before anyone else might spot them or drive them away.

When Devers called to report that the sword was missing, she realized there was no time to lose. Though the curator couldn't verify John's identity, she suspected that he must have been the man who had accompanied Hillary into the vault and then escaped with the sword.

Cynthia knew John wanted to help the mermaids, but she hadn't really imagined him capable of such an impetuous move. It was now a race against time to see who could reach the Merrow Rocks first. If John beat her to the creatures, and broke the enchantment, there would be nothing left for her to study.

After several frantic phone calls, she and her team of graduate students, including Hillary (who, despite a headache and some mild nausea, was none the worse for wear), along with Mr. Devers (who felt responsible for the sword's disappearance) all met aboard the research boat that she had chartered.

The storm had not yet blown over, so when Cynthia had insisted that they set out immediately, the captain warned against it, "We can't go out in a squall like this. We need to wait at least another hour for the waves to die down."

Frustrated by the delay, Cynthia began ordering her assistants to don their life preservers and inventory their equipment. In addition to state of the art photographic equipment, she had come armed with nets and tranquilizer harpoons.

"Just what are you planning to look for?" Hillary asked her.

"Something that could be the most important discovery in marine biology in a millennium."

"But you're an archeologist, not a biologist."

"Yes, but what I'm looking for may hold the answer to the origins of the Viking's sword. Don't pester me with questions," Cynthia snorted with irritation. "You don't have to come along."

"Of course I'm coming. I just wish I understood why you are so intent on going out there."

"Almost every legend, including the legend of that sword, has its roots in something real, Hillary. I'm going after those roots."

As the day wore on the rain and wind began to let up. The waves crashing against the beach were no longer so high or so violent. Eventually the sun peeped out around banks of still heavy clouds. After incessant cajoling from Cynthia, the captain at last agreed to take the boat out on the water.

Cynthia scanned the horizon with a pair of binoculars as they approached the Merrow Rocks, hoping to get a glimpse of one of the strange creatures she had sighted before.

She was not disappointed. Several mermaids were perched atop the rocks, sunning themselves. They seemed unaware of the approaching boat. Apparently, either John hadn't yet reached them with the enchanted sword, or it had failed to break the spell.

"Hillary, quick! Make sure you are getting this on film," Cynthia shouted.

Their boat was getting very close now. At any moment, Cynthia expected the creatures to dive out of view, but they remained still, watching.

"David, get that tranquilizer harpoon ready," Cynthia instructed another grad student. "If they dive into the water, shoot as quickly as possible."

Cynthia couldn't believe her luck. Three of the mermaids dove from the rocks and began swimming toward their boat.

"Lower the nets carefully," she ordered. "We mustn't startle them."

David gave a long, low whistle. "No one's ever going to believe this."

"That's why we've got to capture one alive," Cynthia whispered.

*****

No sooner had the wind and rain begun to let up, than John darted from his parked car, clutching the bundled sword to his body. He jumped aboard his boat, stowing the sword carefully. Then, paying no heed to the still pounding surf, he cast off and motored straight for the Merrow Rocks. Long before John reached the rocks, he saw the figure of a lone mermaid, approaching his boat very fast. He adjusted the motor to slow the boat down as she intercepted his path. It was Cliona.

"John! Go back!" she shouted.

"But I have it. I've brought the sword," he replied, pulling the great weapon free from its wrappings.

"They will sink you!"

"Who?"

"Muirna and the others. They are wary of humans now. They will destroy any who come too near."

"But now that we have the sword, they can be set free from the spell. They will be human again, and they won't have to risk being captured."

"Muirna no longer believes so. We are not young women, John. We have lived many hundreds of years beyond our natural life span. It could be that using the sword will end our lives. She and the others don't want to take that risk. They say we must flee back to the open ocean."

In his heart, John knew that he could never bear to be parted from Cliona. He couldn't watch her dive beneath the waves, never to return to him again.

"I know what I shall do," he said firmly. "I will use the sword to transform myself into a merman. Then, at least we will always be together."

"No! You must not!"

"But I love you, Cliona."

"Dearest John, do you not see? I used the sword, long ago, out of fear. I sought to protect myself from the heartbreaks which are the lot of women, and thus I became less than a woman. I could never bear it if I knew that for my sake you had become less than a man."

"Then what am I to do?"

"Take the risk and break the spell."

"But what if you don't survive?"

"Then I will die in your arms. I will enter into eternal rest in the presence of my blessed Lord. I will be reunited with my mother and grandmother, rejoicing before the throne of God. Bury my bones beneath the good, green earth in the land where I was born. I would give anything just to be at rest, to go home to heaven and wander the seas no more... "

With tears in his eyes, John pulled her up into the boat. He held her in his arms and kissed her gently, then he drew out the sword.

"If it goes badly, will you forgive me?" he asked.

She nodded. Closing her eyes, she said, "John, do it quickly."

He thrust the sword through her tail, and with one swift motion, cut down the length of the scaly bonds which had held her for so long. A silvery membrane fell away, to reveal her white legs. Cliona let out a low cry and fainted.

John took his overcoat and wrapped it around her. He cradled her close to his chest. When he felt her warm breath against his cheek, he began to weep for joy.

*****

Cynthia watched with glee as the mermaids moved closer to the boat and the nets they had lowered. The creatures began chanting a wild, rhythmic song.

Cynthia and her team were so transfixed, that at first they didn't notice the shaking as something hit the side of the boat. The craft shivered with the vibration.

"We're running aground on the rocks," Hillary exclaimed.

But Cynthia realized that couldn't be true. The pounding on their hull was deliberate and it was continuing in time with the mermaids' chant.

She ran to the far side of the boat and looked down. Below the waterline, there were many more mermaids. They had positioned what appeared to be large, stone axe heads against the hull. Teams of two or three were taking turns slamming these weapons with the full force of their tails.

Cynthia dropped her camera, and hurried below. Water was flooding into the cabin, as the stone wedges ripped through the boat's hull. She grabbed several life preservers which she brought up to the others on deck.

"They are ripping the ship apart. They mean to sink us."

The captain tried to turn the craft, but she was taking on water too fast. He tried radioing for help, but the bad weather interfered with his signals. There was no hope for the little boat.

The stunned voyagers could do nothing but watch as the mermaids continued their assault. The boat foundered and water began pouring over the sides. More mermaids closed in on the terrified research team. They swept the net which had been lowered to capture them up and over the people, then dove for the bottom, dragging their catch behind them.

Cynthia held her breath, trying to struggle free from the nets so that the buoyancy of her life vest might carry her to the surface. Mermaid hands grasped at her ankles, while others sawed through the straps on her life vest with pieces of sharpened shell. It had been folly to think that she could escape from the Sirens with her life, much less capture one. The hunter had become the prey. Cynthia's lifeless body sank to the bottom.

*****

The wreckage from the research vessel couldn't be recovered. Neither could the bodies, which did not surprise Cliona. "My sisters will feed their flesh to the sharks and the orcas," she told John.

John was uneasy about what to do with the enchanted sword, and toyed with the idea of returning it to the museum, but Cliona disagreed.

"It belonged to my people, and though my sisters have chosen to remain in their bonds, there may come a day, even a hundred years from now, when they will grow as weary of their ocean exile as I did."

They sailed out to the Merrow Rocks at sunset, and, with tear stained eyes, Cliona threw the great sword into the depths. John put his arms around her, as she wept on his shoulder.

"I cannot make them choose as I did, but I can at least offer them the power to find their way home."

At the memorial service for those who had been killed in the accident, John introduced Cliona to Bryan,

"I'd like you to meet my fiancé."

Offering his hand, Bryan said, "I always thought John was a confirmed bachelor. I'm so glad he's going to prove me wrong."

Cliona smiled and cast an adoring look at John.

"Wherever did you find her?" Bryan whispered.

"We have a mutual love of sailing," John explained.

"That's great, but don't you think you're robbing the cradle?" Bryan asked.

John smiled. "Actually, she's older than she looks."

Everything He Needed to Say

It was early April and my young daughter and I were preparing to host a tea party in our backyard. I watched the early afternoon sunlight and dappled shade from our mulberry trees play over the emerald grass. *This Saturday's party will be perfect*, I thought as I arranged pretty, purple Irises in baskets for our centerpieces.

The phone rang, shattering my carefree daydreams. It was Karen, my father's wife, calling from Canada. "Becky, I don't know how to tell you this," she began. "Your father is dead."

I sat speechless, unwilling to believe my ears.

"It was a heart attack," Karen explained. Dad had gotten up that morning and gone through his regular routine, eating breakfast, spending time reading the Bible and then praying. "Today, he prayed mostly for the family," she told me. After that, he had walked down the stairs to the basement and just collapsed. By the time medical help could be summoned, he was already dead.

I immediately made plans to travel to Canada for his funeral. Though my father had been absent throughout my childhood, in the few short years I had known him, this man had become dear to me and I wanted to honor his memory.

My mother and father had split up when I was too young to remember him, and I had had no contact with my father until I reached my early twenties. At that point in my life I was torn between wanting to reach out to him, and fear that he might not welcome a relationship with me. He had another wife and children. If I reappeared on the scene, wouldn't it just complicate his life?

Most of my uncertainties were put to rest when he sent me a letter, inviting me and my husband to visit his farm in Saskatchewan, yet I remember my feelings of trepidation as we drove down the rutted, dirt road, past fields of flowering, golden canola, to their tiny Tudor-style farmhouse. How would this stranger who was my father receive me? What would his wife and two teenage daughters think of me?

We were welcomed in and sat down at the kitchen table. My dad grasped my hand between both of his, as though he never wanted to let it go. "O, Becky, it's so good to see you!" he said, again and again, a broad grin beaming from his face. I looked around the table at Karen and the girls whose faces were alight with the same bright smiles, and felt all of my hesitations melt away in the warmth of their joy.

From that time on, my dad was faithful to call me regularly, just to say "hi," and to tell me he loved me. We had a few more face to face visits over the years. In fact, the fall before his death, he and his wife had driven down to Arizona to stay with us. He came bearing gifts for my children that he had painstakingly handcrafted himself: a red and yellow biplane for my son and a wooden easel for my daughter. My kids treasured this special time with their grandma and grandpa from Canada. None of us even imagined that this would be the last time we would see him alive.

At Dad's funeral, a friend of his made a statement about him that I thought was very profound. "I think Jim had said everything he needed to say," the man told me, "so it was time for him to go home to Heaven." In other words, he didn't have a lot of unfinished business; he hadn't left a lot of things unsaid.

I pondered the man's words and realized that, from my point of view, I had to agree. Even though my dad's death was so sudden and unexpected, and we had not really had a chance to say goodbye, I had no lingering doubts about his feelings for me. He had sought reconciliation with me. He had made a special effort to build relationships with my children, and he had been faithful to express his love for me again and again in the few years that we had.

Other people also bore witness to the fact that my dad had said what he needed to say to them, even when they didn't want to hear it. After the funeral, my sisters' band teacher from high school came by the house to offer his condolences. He mentioned that Dad had told him straightforwardly that he needed to get right with God. Even though the band teacher had made it clear to Dad that he "wasn't buying," Karen said he still went out of his way to seek Dad's company at social gatherings, even when he was half-drunk, though he knew Dad didn't approve.

My dad shot straight with people and they respected him for it, whether they liked the things he had to say or not. He did not allow the awkwardness of never having spoken to me as a child intimidate him into continued silence. Instead, he overcame that barrier in order to tell me again and again how much he loved me. Life is fragile. None of us knows which day will be our last, and that is why the life lesson my dad taught me is so important. Dad said everything he needed to say. I hope that when my life is through, the same can be said of me.

ABOUT THE AUTHOR

Rebecca D. Bruner
A Fresh Voice for Timeless Truths

Author and speaker Rebecca D. Bruner has been a leader in women's ministries for more than twenty years. In addition to the short stories included in this collection, Rebecca has published two works of Biblical fiction: *Mary's Perfume* and *Sarah's Laughter*. She has recently been elected vice president of Christian Writers of the West, the local chapter of American Christian Fiction Writers, and also serves as the secretary for her Mesa Christian Writers' critique group Rebecca is a passionate Bible teacher who has taught Bible studies for at risk women and girls through Hope Women's Center, and has spoken at several women's retreats and conferences, including the Women 4 Truth 2012 conference. She currently serves as a mentor and speaker for Faith Church of the Valley's Moms Connect mentoring ministry. Her husband and two teenagers keep her very busy, but she loves every minute of it.

www.RebeccaBruner.wordpress.com

www.facebook.com/RebeccaBrunerAuthor

Made in the USA
Charleston, SC
19 January 2013